SEARCH FOR T

SEARCH FOR THE FOX

Stephen Overholser

Chivers Press • G.K. Hall & Co.
Bath, Avon, England • Thorndike, Maine USA

This Large Print edition is published by Chivers Press, England, and by
G.K. Hall & Co., USA.

Published in 1996 in the U.K. by arrangement with the author.

Published in 1996 in the U.S. by arrangement with Golden West Literary
Agency.

U.K. Hardcover ISBN 0–7451–4944–8 (Chivers Large Print)
U.K. Softcover ISBN 0–7451–4955–3 (Camden Large Print)
U.S. Softcover ISBN 0–7838–1850–5 (Nightingale Collection Edition)

The text of this Large Print edition is unabridged.
Other aspects of the book may vary from the original edition.

Set in 16 pt. New Times Roman.

Printed in Great Britain on acid-free paper.

British Library Cataloguing in Publication Data available

Library of Congress Cataloging-in-Publication Data

Overholser, Stephen.
    Search for the Fox / Stephen Overholser.
        p. cm.
    ISBN 0–7838–1850–5 (lg. print : sc)
    1. Large type books.   I. Title.
[PS3565.V43S4   1996]
813′.54—dc20

96–20902

To my brothers,
John and Daniel

CHAPTER ONE

John Fox, the outlaw, was my father. My search for him in the West began after the death of my mother. Before my journey was over, I came to know that my true search was for myself.

During the War Between the States, my father was known as the Fox. He had earned fame and quick promotions because of his ability in leading a small band of Southern volunteers against large numbers of Union regulars, and routing them. At a time when hope was most needed, John Fox gave it. By war's end he was the youngest general officer in the army of the South.

At the time of the surrender, I was a few months old. In that year my father, still in uniform and making no attempt to cover his well-known face, rode into Richmond and robbed the Atlantic Bank & Trust. He fled the South, leaving his wife and infant son behind. In a short time General John Fox became notorious in the West as Fox, the outlaw.

Summer 1882 was near the end of my seventeenth year. I was at my mother's bedside, holding her small hand in both of mine. Never before had I realized how small her hand was, and how frail. Years later a man wrote in a book of local history that Mother died of a broken heart. As with many other fanciful things that have been written about my family, that is untrue. Mother died of consumption. I watched her die. And I listened to her last words.

Black Mattie stood at the foot of the bed, sobbing. She had fretted endlessly over Mother, running in and out of the master bedroom with pans of steaming water for the 'vapors' that Mother was supposed to breathe.

Now Mother raised up on an elbow. She scolded Mattie and told her to leave the room. The big woman left reluctantly, threatening to send for Dr Renfrew herself. I heard her mumbling unhappily as she walked down the hall and descended the wide staircase.

Mother sat up in bed and pointed to the fireplace. 'Benjamin, lift out the bricks from the hearth there.'

Though her request was strange, I knew this was no time to question her. I went to the fireplace. Kneeling by the hearth, I removed the soot-covered bricks. To my surprise I uncovered a strongbox. I had spent nearly every day of my seventeen years in the Fox mansion. Until now I had thought I knew every nook and cranny.

'Bring it here, Benjamin,' Mother said.

I lifted the strongbox out, wiped the soot off, and brought it to Mother's bedside. She told me the key to the lock was in the bottom of her jewelry case, then sank back to her pillows. I

2

found the key and used it to open the strongbox.

Inside I found a gold pocket watch and two thousand dollars in Union currency. The money itself was a small scandal to my mind. We had not only lived frugally in those last years, sending away all the servants but Mattie and her husband Abraham, but Mother was intensely loyal and vocal for the Southern cause. I would not have been surprised to have found the strongbox filled with notes issued by the Confederacy. Many old families proudly kept such money with the idea that it would be good once again. It was a shock to me to discover that Mother had secretly given up the belief.

Mother asked for the gold watch. I put it in her hand. Her fingers folded over it, and she spoke to me in a weak voice.

'Benjamin ... our property ... all of it ... will be sold to pay off the debts. I have decided to leave you without land ... and without debts. Judge Madison will execute my will and see to everything. The money in the box is all I have to leave you, Benjamin. Speak to no one of it ... not even the judge ... or it will be taken from you as a part of the estate.'

Mother began to cry softly. She wondered what would become of me. I said I would be all right, that she should think only of herself and of recovering. But she said:

'I'll not live the night, Benjamin.'

3

I rushed out of the bedroom and found Mattie. I told her to send Abraham to Richmond for the doctor and Judge Madison.

Mother's instincts were true. Within the hour she grew delirious and began to ramble in her speech. She became fearful of being left alone. I reassured her of my presence.

For a time Mother came to her senses. She insisted that I put the currency in my pocket where no one could see it. Then she told me to set the strongbox back in the hearth and replace the bricks. She watched me do so, and called me back to her bedside.

Mother handed the gold watch to me and told me to open it. The outside of the cover was engraved with a hunting scene, showing a man with a shotgun who had just flushed a covey of birds. I pressed the release on the side of the watch. The cover sprang open. Inside, opposite the face of the watch, was a small copy of Mother and Father's wedding portrait. I knew Mother kept a larger, framed copy of the photograph in her dresser. The picture was kept hidden from me there, as was the memory of my father. But on several occasions over the years when I had come into the bedroom without knocking, I had found Mother gazing into that photograph as though trying to enter it.

Now I looked at the small portrait in the watch cover. It was hardly larger than a postage stamp, but the figures were as clear as life. John Fox was a young man in 1864, the year of his marriage, and he was very handsome in his gray dress uniform. He stood beside a young girl who stared soberly out of the photograph at me. Now, barely past her youth, that girl was dying.

Soon Mother worsened and again rambled about things that made little sense to me, but troubled me. She said she was deserving of her fate. And of the gold pocket watch, she said repeatedly that I must return it to my father, and he must be told of her sorrow and regret.

Mother's request was not rational for we did not know where my father was. We did not want to know where he was. John Fox was a dishonored man, a man who had earned a fine reputation and had thrown it away by committing a crime.

Mother passed on that night before either the doctor or Judge Madison could arrive. To the end she murmured senselessly about my father and about her own sins. She begged me to return the watch to him. I promised I would, but my voice seemed not to reach her. She was not consoled, and at last I was left holding her lifeless hand in both of mine.

*   *   *

Judge Horatio Madison was a big, silver-haired man with a long beard that was combed straight down to the center of his chest. In 1882 he was nearing seventy, yet in my memory he had not aged at all. He was hardy and strong now as he always had been and, I believed, always would be.

Judge Madison had not served on the bench for more than a decade, but he looked like the kind of man who should. His dark eyes seemed to possess fire and peer into the heart of every man or question that came to his attention. Since childhood, I had believed he could look into my eyes and read my thoughts.

I had been educated by Judge Madison. Even though I knew him well, I had never felt close to him, and I had never overcome my youthful fear of him. He was over-powering. As a teacher he was capable of great wrath. If I made a mistake in my lessons, I braced myself for his thunderous voice. Was I without wits? Why should he waste his time with me? At this I would always redouble my efforts and try to gain his favor, for being in the favor of Judge Madison was like basking in sunshine.

My mother always knew how well or how poorly I was doing in my studies. Judge Madison was her lifelong friend and adviser. During my early childhood they made the decision that I would not be educated in public schools, but would be tutored privately. Judge Madison agreed to take on this task.

Mother reminded me often of this good luck. She could not afford to pay a full-time tutor of the judge's standing, and he had consented to undertake my education at no expense. Since Mother never remarried, and the judge spent a great deal of time with us, Mother encouraged me to think of him as both a teacher and a father.

Mother used her dwindling fortune to hire a few tutors on a part-time basis. These were men who could educate me in the 'manly arts.' Judge Madison followed this part of my education with much interest, too, for he believed that while a young gentleman must learn the rules set down by the marquis of Queensbury, he must also, for self-protection, learn to be aggressive with a knife or saber, a pistol, and a rifle.

I became skilled with these weapons after many hours of drills and practice on the remainder of the Fox estate. I had few boyhood friends, and I would often practice my lessons alone after my tutor had left for the day. At times I would ride my horse, Sun King, into battle with imaginary enemies, riding alongside General John Fox. We would charge together and send the enemy into wild retreat.

Though I knew the family fortune was no longer great, I was never made aware of our dire circumstances. The fact that my few private tutors was a luxury was something I never gave thought to. In truth, hiring tutors would have defied anyone else's sense of practicality—anyone but my mother's, that is. For three generations her people had been

7

educated in this manner. No son of hers would be forced to endure a 'common' education.

At the time I accepted this as wisdom rather than as impracticality. It was only after I embarked on my search for the Fox that I came to know what a sheltered life I had led. Other boys my age ran through the streets of Richmond and the surrounding countryside in joyful packs. Whenever I was in town, usually with Mother or with the judge, I had remained aloof from these yelling, undisciplined boys.

*   *   *

I heard Dr Renfrew come hurrying up the staircase. Two days ago he had visited Mother and said her illness was not serious. Now he hurried to her bedside. Judge Madison was only minutes behind, as were Mattie and Abraham. Mattie began to cry as soon as she entered the room.

'She's gone, Judge,' Dr Renfrew said.

The doctor pulled the bedsheet over Mother's white face. I reached out and jerked the bedsheet back, glancing angrily at the doctor, then at Judge Madison. He looked struck.

'She was so young,' he said hoarsely.

Dr Renfrew lifted Mother's hand from mine. He tried to lead me away from the bed. I refused to go. Mother had begged me not to leave her. At last Judge Madison cleared his throat and came around the bed. He placed his hand on my shoulder.

'Come with me, Benjamin,' he said.

I stayed the night in Judge Madison's house in town. The following afternoon we buried my mother. Many of the old families of Virginia came to the services. Mother's relatives were there, as well as some of the Foxes, people I had rarely seen.

Afterward I lingered behind, staying longer even than Mattie and Abraham. I could not pull my eyes away from the fresh grave. The headstone bore a message I was only beginning to believe. In my mind I still heard Mother's last pleas.

Judge Madison called to me from his buggy, 'Benjamin, we must go.'

I turned away from the grave and looked at him. Long shafts of afternoon sunlight slanted through the trees that marked the edge of the cemetery. One shone upon Judge Madison as he sat in his one-horse buggy. This trick of light made his hair and beard look all the more silvery, his gaze all the more piercing. Despite my mother's suggestion, I had never been able to think of him as a father. Instead I had long held the belief that he looked like God, or at least God would be proud to look that way. And like God, I both feared and loved Judge Madison.

In silence I rode with this man back to his house in Richmond.

9

CHAPTER TWO

Early that evening Judge Madison called me into his study. From his tone of voice I knew a serious talk was at hand. I stood before his huge oak desk, like a defendant before the bench, and respectfully kept my hands at my sides, as I had been taught.

Judge Madison began by asking if I was aware of my present financial circumstances. I said I was. But as I spoke, my mind was rocked when I remembered the money Mother had left me. For the first time in my life I had knowledge of an important family matter that Judge Madison did not even suspect, something I could never tell him. This knowledge had the effect of a revelation on me. As I stood before Judge Madison that evening I suddenly saw him for what he was: a silver-haired, bearded man, not a god.

'Benjamin, there may be a few hundred dollars left from the sale of the property. Your mother sold off the best tobacco acreage over the years. The remaining land is mortgaged to the hilt. The debts have grown deeper and deeper, I'm afraid.'

Mother sold choice tobacco land from the original Fox estate on Judge Madison's advice. I noticed he made no mention of that now.

'This leaves you in a predicament, Benjamin.

You know your mother's dream was for you to enter a school of higher education and study the law. I daresay you have a proper background for such study.' He paused.

I caught his hint and said, 'Yes, sir.'

'You do not have the funds for such an education,' Judge Madison went on, 'nor do you have the background to seek employment in any recognized field of endeavor—except, perhaps, teaching. I know your mother would want you to seek more dignified employment than that. So do I. You were raised as a gentleman, and I want to see you become one.'

At his pause I replied again, 'Yes, sir.'

'Therefore, I am prepared to give you the financial aid, on loan at 4 per cent interest, that you will require to complete a study of the law. Can you be ready to start in the fall?'

'Yes, sir,' I said, suddenly realizing that he was not asking me a question at all, but was telling me what I would do.

Judge Madison leaned back in his swivel chair and studied me. 'I know this is a day of sorrow for you, Benjamin, but have you nothing else to say?'

'Yes, sir,' I said quickly, 'thank you for your generous offer.'

'You accept it, don't you?'

I began to nod, as a reflex, then I shook my head. My throat drew tight and my voice squeaked when I said, 'Sir, I am going to search for my father.'

11

That was the nearest I had ever come to defying Judge Madison. I braced myself for his reply, expecting an explosion. But his face went slack and he spoke in a low voice:

'I forbid it.'

I watched him leave his chair and cross the study. He stopped at the bay window overlooking his flower garden. With his broad back to me, he said:

'Where did you get this notion?'

I realized that if I told him what Mother had said to me from her deathbed, Judge Madison would tell me what I already knew. Her final request was irrational. Had she been well she never would have made the plea.

I said, 'It has been on my mind for a long time, sir.'

'I was afraid of this,' Judge Madison said. He turned to face me. 'Benjamin, John Fox cast dishonor upon himself and upon the Fox name. He chose the wrong path of life.'

I had heard him say that before. Now the words sounded pious and explained nothing.

'He was a hero during the war, sir.'

'No one can argue that,' Judge Madison said. 'John Fox was a gifted leader. Men would follow him to the gates of hell. In the war, men did. But, Benjamin, that only serves to emphasize the magnitude of his criminal act. For an honorable man to cast away his honor in favor of criminal behavior is the worst of sins.'

I grew impatient with the old judge. It occurred to me now that John Fox was not here to defend himself.

'I want to find him,' I said. 'I want to hear his side of it.'

My remark brought the old man's rage to the surface. 'Do you doubt me, Benjamin?'

I shook my head.

Judge Madison said sharply, 'When John Fox ran off from your mother, you were nothing but an infant, a helpless infant.'

I nodded, wishing I had not angered him so.

'Benjamin, when the war was over John Fox came here, here to this very room. He attempted to rob me. You didn't know that, did you, Benjamin? John Fox held his revolver to my head and threatened me with my life. When he found that I kept no money here, he robbed the bank. Richmond was in ruin. Our defenses were down. The only law was provided haphazardly by the Yankees. John Fox took advantage of the situation. He used his wartime skills to rob—'

'But why?' I asked. 'Why did he do it?'

'John Fox needed money,' Judge Madison said bitterly. 'He was young and ambitious. He was a war hero, yet he had received no pay for months. The same was true of thousands of other soldiers. But John Fox believed he could take whatever he wanted—as he had in the war. He became a servant of greed. The result was he had to flee. He left his young wife and

13

baby behind.'

'I didn't know he tried to rob you,' I said.

'I'm sorry I had to tell you, Benjamin,' he said. 'Your mother and I have tried to protect you from his crimes so you would not be tarred by the same brush. You see, John Fox thought I was a rich man. He accused me of profiteering during the war. His accusations were false, of course. Like many other men, I lost everything.'

I said, 'He must have loved my mother.'

Judge Madison shook his head slowly. 'How can you believe that?'

I don't think he expected me to answer the question. I had no answer. It was only Mother's rambling talk during her last hour of life that made me understand how little I knew of what really happened between them back in 1865. All I knew was what Judge Madison had told me.

'I forbid you to undertake a search for John Fox, Benjamin.'

'I must, sir,' I said.

Judge Madison slapped his hand on the polished desktop. The sound was like a shot. 'Then you may expect no help from me in the future—of any kind.' He stared me down. 'You're throwing your life away, Benjamin.'

'I can't rest until I find my father,' I said.

Judge Madison turned away from me and looked out the bay window. A long silence passed between us. In a voice so low that I barely heard him, he said, 'Is that all that's bothering you?'

I was mystified by the remark. 'What?'

His lips moved to form a word, then stopped. In that moment I had the feeling, as a boy often does, that an adult was on the verge of saying something important, giving a message that would allow a boy a glimpse into the mysteries of adulthood; but then the adult thinks better of it and goes on to say something else.

'I have told you of John Fox,' Judge Madison said. 'Do you doubt what I say?'

'No, sir.'

'Then what is it?' he demanded. 'What compels you to undertake this search?'

I did not know how to put my feelings into words. I wanted to tell him that my father lived only in my imagination, that I felt incomplete. But all I could think to say was:

'I want to hear his voice.'

'This is foolishness, Benjamin.'

Out of nervousness I thrust my hands into my trouser pockets. One hand touched the gold watch Mother had given me.

Judge Madison asked, 'How do you propose to find a man like John Fox?'

'A newspaper article said he was in Colorado,' I said.

Judge Madison laughed harshly. 'When the scoundrel robbed a train? That was over a year ago. It is unlikely he stayed around there for

15

long. Do you intend to wander about the state of Colorado?'

Again I had no answer to his question. The truth was I had not thought that far ahead. I knew I could find my father, that was all.

'What if John Fox is in California?' Judge Madison asked. 'Or Montana? Or Texas? Benjamin, a man who lives outside the law must keep moving. He must cover his tracks. John Fox appears to be an expert at that. In all these years he has never been captured and sent to prison where he belongs.'

'I know I can find him, sir,' I said.

'No, you don't,' Judge Madison countered. 'That is precisely the point I am making. You are very young. You have led a protected life. Everything has been laid out for you since the day of your birth. What makes you think you can survive out there?' He waved toward the bay window.

His challenge stung me. It was true that I had never proved myself. I had an education, but had never used it. I had learned of fighting, but had never fought. Perhaps I had lived for seventeen years without ever having truly lived.

I turned away from Judge Madison and moved to the door of the study.

'Benjamin,' Judge Madison said, 'walk out that door now and you will be forsaking all that your mother and I have done for you. Leave my house now, Benjamin, and I will not

16

allow you back in. Give deep thought to what you are about to do.'

I was surprised to hear an undertone of desperation in his voice. I remembered seeing him at the cemetery that afternoon and thinking that God must look like him. I realized now that was only a child's dream. Judge Madison was a man, and an old one. He was losing me, the boy he had educated and practically raised. I felt saddened by what I saw, but determined, too.

'I won't shame you, sir,' I said, and walked out of the study and out of Judge Madison's house.

CHAPTER THREE

That night I packed my saddlebags with the few clothes and personal items I would need. In the morning I planned to catch the earliest westbound train out of Richmond.

I would take Sun King, the gelding I had raised from a colt. The horse's coat shone a beautiful yellow-gold in the sunlight. I'd had several offers from buyers who were prepared to buy Sun King on looks alone. But he had more than looks. He had strength and endurance. I would need him when I reached Colorado.

Taking the horse was probably illegal. Sun

King was a part of the estate and was due to be sold at auction. I hoped to be long gone before he was missed. Late in that last night in my own bed a curious thought came to my mind. If I was breaking a law by leaving with the horse, then I was following my father's example.

I packed my Bowie knife and revolver in my saddlebags. The revolver, an old-model .41-caliber six-shooter, had an octagonal twelve-inch barrel. Though it was old and clumsy for a handgun, it was very accurate and had long range.

After much practice I became a marksman with both the revolver and my repeating rifle. The tutors drilled me, requiring many hours of target shooting. One tutor worked very hard to teach me hand-to-hand combat with the Bowie knife, but I never mastered the weapon as well as I had the firearms.

Of the money Mother left me, I put half into an envelope. Most of what was left went into the money belt that I would wear beneath my shirt.

It was long after nightfall when I left the mansion and walked through the oak grove to the Negro cabin. I knocked on the door and entered when I heard Mattie's voice.

As I expected, I found her sitting in her rocker near the wood stove. At this time of night old Abraham would be back in the small bedroom, asleep. I had spent many hours in this cabin, sitting on the floor in front of the big stove. The stove doors were decorated with metal leaves and vines encircling a puffy-cheeked, cheerful face. The open mouth of the face blew cast-iron clouds across the oven door. I had often stared into this face while Mattie entertained me with her lively stories. They were told to me at those times when Mother was busy with guests or when she and Judge Madison were busy discussing business matters and did not want a boy underfoot.

Mattie was a grand story-teller. Like an actress, she could change her voice to fit the many characters in her stories. All of the characters lived vividly in my imagination, and I could have described any of them in detail if I had been asked. Most of Mattie's stories came from the Bible. A few were tales she remembered hearing as a child, and these were about Africans with strange-sounding names.

As I stood before Mattie that night, the memories of the past rushed into my mind, and I felt a sudden and deep sense of loss. My boyhood was gone. And in all those years Mattie had been a second mother to me. Now I had come to tell her that this land was being sold out from under her.

Mattie listened to me and nodded slowly as she rocked in her chair. 'We knowed it, little Ben. We knowed Miz Fox was on hard times.'

'I wish it weren't so,' I said.

'We'll make do, me and Abe,' Mattie said. 'Don't you worry over us.' She fell silent, then

19

looked up at me. 'What's to come of you, little Ben? You going to Richmond?'

'I'm leaving for Colorado in the morning,' I said.

'Colorado?' Mattie exclaimed. 'What for?'

'I'm going to look for my father,' I said.

'John Fox?' Mattie said. 'Why do you want to find him?'

'I want to ask him why he left us,' I said.

Mattie laughed softly. 'I can tell you that. He left because he done robbed the bank in Richmond.'

'I know,' I said. 'I want to find out why he did it.'

'He needed money, I reckon,' Mattie said. 'Does the judge know you're going out West?'

'Yes,' I said.

'And he's letting you go off on your own?' Mattie asked.

'It is something I have to do,' I said.

Mattie must have sensed that there had been a conflict between Judge Madison and me. 'My, you have growed. You're bound and determined to find things out for yourself, ain't you?'

I nodded.

Mattie smiled. 'Yes, you're going to find things out.'

I reached into my pocket and brought out the envelope. I handed it to her.

'What's this?' Mattie asked. She opened it. 'Why, little Ben, where'd you get all this

20

money?'

'Mother left it to you and Abraham,' I said.

'I can't take this money.' Mattie thrust the envelope at me, but I stepped away.

I had known I would have to lie to make her accept it. 'You have to take it, Mattie. It was Mother's last wish.'

Mattie sighed and began rocking in her chair.

I said, 'You and Abe should stay here until you find out who buys the estate. If an old family buys it, maybe you can stay on. Or maybe you can go to Richmond and work for Judge Madison.'

Mattie shook her head, but said nothing. I watched her lean forward and stand. She came to me and put her big arms around me.

'You go on, now,' she whispered. 'You go on and find John Fox.'

I opened the cabin door and turned back and said goodbye. Mattie held the envelope in her hand. She waved for me to leave. She was crying soundlessly.

I walked back to the mansion, thinking of what I was leaving behind and trying to imagine what lay ahead. I knew I would sleep very little that night.

In the gray light of dawn I walked to the stables and saddled Sun King. I rode around the grounds of the Fox estate, letting Sun King kick up his heels and work out his kinks.

At sunup I returned to the mansion. I took a

last walk through it, lingering at the door of Mother's bedroom. Then I left, half running down the long hall and the stairs. I mounted Sun King and rode to the front gate at a gallop.

I opened the gate and turned and looked back. The lane was bordered by tall hedges. They had been trimmed by Abraham ever since I could remember. From here the mansion's white columns and large, dark windows were framed in sculptured greenery. I wondered if I would ever see this sight again.

I heard the sounds of an approaching buggy. I pulled Sun King around and rode into a break in the hedge. Through a screen of branches and leaves I saw Judge Madison turn his one-horse buggy into the lane and drive past. He did not see me. I caught a glimpse of his face. He looked haggard, as though he had spent a sleepless night, too.

I did not call out or follow him down the lane. I was certain he had come here to renew our argument. Perhaps he had regrets and wanted to apologize. But I knew we had both spoken our minds. For me there was nothing left to say.

I rode Sun King through the hedge, turned, and rode out the open gate. When I reached the main road, I let the horse run. The morning air was warm and sweet, and it roared past my ears all the way to the depot in Richmond.

I bought a train ticket that morning, the first of many, and made arrangements to have Sun

King loaded in a stock car. I boarded one of the passenger coaches and found a seat by the window just as the train whistle blew. The train pulled away from the depot and quickly built up speed. Within four hours I was farther away from home than I had ever been before.

During the next week Sun King and I became experienced train travelers. Many of the trains were small and ran only a few miles. I would have to get off and wait for another. Sometimes the wait was several hours. As I soon learned that many train crewmen had no patience with animals, I got into the practice of loading and unloading Sun King myself.

I rode the many small main lines and feeder lines through the South and the farm country of the Midwest, moving in the general direction of Kansas City. I was anxious to get there because I would board my last train. The Union Pacific line ran straight to Denver.

At first the stop-and-go train travel was exciting, but after three days and three nearly sleepless nights, I was tired and trainsick. I lost my appetite and most of my humor.

At last I arrived at the busy train yards of Kansas City. Following the ticket clerk's directions, I found my train and led Sun King to a stock car near the caboose. After loading him, I boarded a passenger coach.

I found an empty pair of seats and sat on the aisle side. One of the first things I had learned about train travel was that my legs were too

23

long and my feet were too big to be comfortable in a chair by the window. I got in the habit of sitting by the aisle where I could stretch out.

I watched the passengers board as the coach quickly filled. Many people lifted packages and valises to the racks overhead. A fat lady waddled along the aisle. She came toward me like a ship through a narrow channel, pushing aside the unfortunate passengers who were in her way and leaving them behind in her wake.

The fat lady's head was covered by a large hat with a long-plumed feather trailing out behind, the kind of hat that might make someone sneeze if he got too close. She stopped by the empty pair of seats across the aisle from me. I saw her turn and move in, lower herself, and then adjust her bulk into the chair by the window.

I was staring at the fat lady and did not see the girl until the girl spoke to me in an irritable way:

'Won't you help me?'

I looked up and then got to my feet. The girl was honey-haired and blue-eyed. I guessed she was about my age. I could not take my eyes from her, and when I finally mumbled that I would be glad to help her, she shook her head and pointed down the aisle.

'Not me. My father.'

A slender man wearing a stovepipe hat slowly made his way up the aisle. He carried two leather valises that appeared to be too heavy for him. I went to him and offered to take them.

The man smiled gratefully. He removed his hat. Fine beads of sweat shone on his forehead. One of the valises was heavy. I carried both and followed the man back to the girl. She had taken the window seat next to mine. As I lifted the valises to the rack overhead, I heard the girl say:

'Here, Father, sit here.'

The man thanked me again, then gently collapsed into the seat that had been mine. The girl avoided looking at me by giving her full attention to her father. The train whistle blew. I looked around the coach. The only seat left was on the aisle, next to the fat lady.

CHAPTER FOUR

The train bound for Denver rolled out of the Kansas City rail yards. The uniformed conductor came through the swaying coach, punching passengers' tickets. After he had punched mine and passed by, the girl's father reached across the aisle and tapped my arm.

'My name is Collier Moore, Dr Collier Moore.'

I shook his hand. 'I'm Benjamin Fox.'

Dr Collier Moore leaned back in his seat,

25

giving me full view of his daughter. 'Benjamin, this is my daughter, Casey. I take it you two have met, but I'll introduce you formally. Casey, meet Benjamin Fox.'

Casey Moore glanced at me, barely nodded, then looked out her window as though interested in the passing scenery. The train was rolling through a shanty town on the fringe of Kansas City.

'Are you headed for Denver, Benjamin?' Dr Collier Moore asked.

'Yes, sir,' I said. His voice was deep and commanding. I sensed he was a man who would be determined to learn all he could about whomever he met. I did not want to tell anyone why I was going to Colorado, but I was certain Dr Collier Moore was on the verge of asking.

'Well,' he asked, 'will you make your fortune there?'

I smiled. 'Yes, sir.'

'That's the spirit,' Dr Collier Moore said. His deep voice boomed over the monotonous sounds of the coach's wheels clicking over the rails. 'Casey and I are headed for Cloud City, Colorado. Perhaps we'll make our fortunes there, too. Cloud City is the greatest silver-producing region in the world now. There seems to be no end to the riches there.'

I listened politely, but I looked at Casey. She avoided looking at me.

'Not that I'm a miner,' Dr Collier Moore

said. 'I'm going to Cloud City for reasons of health. The altitude there is over ten thousand feet above the seas. The rarefied air will be beneficial to my health, I'm told.'

Now the fat lady beside me leaned forward and spoke across me. 'Pardon me, sir, but I can keep my silence no longer. Are you *the* Dr Collier Moore?'

He was obviously pleased at being recognized. 'I believe I am, madam.'

I tried to lean away from the fat lady's pressing warmth, but she only leaned closer. At this range I saw a powdered mustache across her upper lip and I could not escape her sour breath.

'My sister attended your lecture series in Philadelphia last winter. She simply raved over you. She told me you changed her life.'

'I am gratified to hear that, madam,' he said.

The fat lady breathed heavily with her excitement. 'I am a believer in the wonders of phrenology, too. Science of the mind is a future trend. Will you lecture in Denver?'

Until now I had thought Dr Collier Moore was a medical doctor. I had seen only one other phrenologist in my life. Mother had great faith in the man's ability to examine the human skull and learn hidden details of a person's character and strengths and weaknesses. Judge Madison, however, called them 'bumpologists.' He said they were all soft-headed quacks who advocated wild social causes like trial marriage and mixing the races.

To the fat lady Dr Collier Moore repeated his plans to go to Cloud City for reasons of health. The fat lady was shocked.

'Cloud City is nothing but a rough mining camp, doctor,' she said. 'You will find no civilization there at all. No law, either, but the law of the jungle. Did you know there is a murder in Cloud City every day?'

Dr Collier Moore smiled. He said he had heard such wild stories, but he discounted them. He had received correspondence from a friend in Cloud City who said there was little truth to them. Dr Collier Moore said he expected a mining camp to be 'spirited.'

'Spirited!' the fat lady exclaimed. 'Lawless is more like it. Dr Moore, you should come to Denver and settle there. In Denver you will find real gentlemen, and ladies who are real ladies. A man of your talents would be appreciated there.'

'Denver is too low in altitude for me,' he said.

'Why, it's a mile high,' the fat lady said.

'That isn't high enough,' Dr Collier Moore said. 'I must live over ten thousand feet above the seas. Doctor's orders, I'm afraid.'

'My, oh, my,' the fat lady said.

Dr Collier Moore had noticed my uncomfortable position. The more I leaned away from the fat lady, the more she leaned into me. Dr Collier Moore asked if he might

28

join her. She said she would be delighted and practically threw me from the seat. Dr Collier Moore and I exchanged seats. He winked at me as he passed by.

Casey stared out of her window at the flat, treeless scenery that steadily slid past. I stretched my feet into the aisle and closed my eyes. The fat lady had told Dr Collier Moore her name was Miss Guffey. They spoke loudly to one another.

'Some say Cloud City is destined to become the capital of Colorado,' Dr Collier Moore said. 'Some of the wealthiest men in the country reside there.'

Miss Guffey replied scornfully. 'You can take my word that Cloud City is nothing but an encampment of dirty miners and ruffians and gamblers and painted women.'

Their voices began to drone along with the rhythmic sounds of the wheels on the rails. I thought of home. It seemed to be far behind in time and space, as though I had left one world and was entering another. My train journey across the Great Plains was like a voyage across an empty sea. I had left the known land where I had grown up. Ahead was a wild, unknown land, a land that concealed my father.

I was wakened by the shrill laughter of Miss Guffey. She and Dr Collier Moore were still deep in conversation. I had slouched down in the upholstered seat. When I straightened up

29

and glanced to the side, my eyes met Casey's.

'You look so innocent in sleep,' she said.

Her impulsive remark embarrassed both of us. At once we tried to laugh, and failed.

'I apologize,' Casey said.

'For what?' I asked.

'For stealing your seat,' she said. 'I shouldn't have done it.'

'Forget it,' I said. 'I have.'

'Thank you,' she said. 'Taking care of my father is a strain—especially this morning.'

'Is he ill?'

'No—yes—' Her voice trailed off. She moved close to me and spoke in a low voice. 'He's impractical. And he's not strong. This morning we were late. We always are. Father can't keep track of time. He doesn't know how to do everyday things, so he leaves them to me. I had to buy the tickets and arrange for the luggage to be loaded into the baggage car. In the meantime, Father got lost.'

Casey cast an irritable glance across the aisle. She whispered to me, 'Why do I always hate the women Father likes?' She immediately grew embarrassed. 'I don't know why I'm saying these things to you.'

I thought I did; she had no one else to confide in. I tried to change the subject of the conversation. 'Your name is unusual, Casey.'

'Cassandra,' she said. 'My father shortened it to Casey.'

I remembered Cassandra from my lessons in

30

Greek mythology. 'Cassandra was given the gift of prophecy by Apollo.'

Casey nodded. 'But it was her fate to never be believed. Wouldn't that be awful: to know what was in the future, but no one would believe you?'

I smiled at her. 'I don't believe in fate. Do you?'

Casey returned my smile. 'No. But I think you're Apollo.'

I laughed. She was more direct than any girl I'd ever talked to. I asked her if she looked forward to living in Cloud City.

Casey shrugged as though the question had no meaning. 'We won't stay long. We never do.'

'Why?'

'Something always happens,' she said. 'In small towns we have to leave after everyone has heard Father's lectures. In the cities we don't stay long because Father always manages to get the wrong people mad at him. Just last month he gave the mayor of Albany, New York, a phrenological reading. Some areas of the man's intellect were not well developed. Well, Father not only told him that, but he went on to speak of the highly developed intellects of the black races.'

'Do you believe in phrenology?' I asked.

'Of course I do,' Casey said. 'All modern people should. Just because I get annoyed with my father doesn't mean I don't respect him and

31

love him. He's a great man, a man of the future.' As if to explain, she added, 'Haven't you ever been angry at your father, Ben?'

Casey did not wait for an answer. She turned away and looked out the window again. I thought she regretted speaking to me in such a frank way.

At the first stop of the day, Dr Collier Moore gave Miss Guffey a phrenological reading. Other passengers in the coach crowded around to watch. Dr Collier Moore asked Miss Guffey to remove her hat, then slowly moved his fingers along her forehead. He lightly pressed his fingertips through Miss Guffey's hair, moving over her head all the way to the back. Miss Guffey smiled in silent excitement.

'You have high moral sentiments,' Dr Collier Moore said. 'You're very honest, but somewhat selfish, too.'

This last remark had the effect of removing Miss Guffey's smile.

'Make no mistake,' Dr Collier Moore said, 'every man or woman can control his weaknesses once they are recognized. All one must do is expand his strengths and contain his weaknesses. With a woman of your high intelligence, Miss Guffey, I suspect you already do that.'

Miss Guffey smiled again, pressing her chin into folds of flesh in her neck. 'At times I suppose I am selfish, Dr Moore. But I try not to be.'

'That's the spirit,' he said.

I glanced at Casey. She smiled wryly at this last exchange, as though she had heard it before. Casey had said her father was not tactful, but she was wrong. He seemed very tactful with women.

'Benjamin,' Dr Collier Moore said, 'would you care to have a reading?'

I shook my head. 'No, thank you.'

'I can see from here you're a doubter,' he said. The other passengers turned to look at me. I felt my face grow warm. Dr Collier Moore went on, 'And from your high brow level, I can see you are brilliant. I'll bet you do well in studies. Turn your head to the left.'

I did so, but felt embarrassed.

'Your faculty of curiosity is well developed, Benjamin,' he said. 'Perhaps it is overdeveloped. If so, it might be a weakness that you should learn to control. Are you certain you do not want a full reading?'

'I'm certain, sir,' I said.

'That's because you're a doubter,' Casey said.

'Now, Casey,' Dr Collier Moore said, 'we must be tolerant.'

Dr Collier Moore asked me to lift one of the valises from the rack overhead. I handed it to him. He opened it and brought out a plaster skull. He used it as a model to demonstrate bumps that indicated certain traits. Then he gave phrenological readings to several of the other passengers at two dollars a head.

That night at the dinner stop I bought a two-week-old copy of a Denver newspaper. In the moving coach I read the paper by lamplight. Much of the front page was devoted to news of the booming silver camp named Cloud City. Late at night a headline near the bottom of the last page caught my eye: FOX GANG WAYLAYS STAGE. I held the newspaper closer to the light and read the article.

PASSENGERS TERRIFIED

The illusive Fox gang has struck again. The Denver-Pueblo stagecoach was held up day before yesterday. The passengers were not robbed, but the strongbox was blown open, terrifying man and beast. The team of horses nearly became runaways but for the strength and skill of the driver, Henry White. The strongbox contained a cash payroll for the Pueblo smelter, owned by the Colorado financier and recent silver baron, Alexander B. Reston.

John Fox and his gang of road agents appear to have known all along of this secret cash shipment. This leads the observer to speculate that someone in the employ of Mr Reston is also in the employ of Mr Fox. Mr Reston purposely avoided shipping the payroll by rail as the Fox gang has stopped southbound trains with regularity.

The passengers, three men and two women, were treated politely by the road agents, but all agreed they were terrified. Henry White made the observation that this robbery should put to rest the common rumor that John Fox was shot to death last winter when he was thought to have been cornered by detectives hired by Mr Reston. White said he watched John Fox direct the gang members as they leveled guns at the passengers and blew open the strongbox.

I read the article twice. When I looked up, I found Casey watching me with curiosity.

'Are you related to that outlaw?' she asked.

I shook my head.

'I'll bet you are,' Casey said. She smiled. 'You're probably going to Colorado to join up with his gang.'

'That's right,' I said. 'Hand over your jewelry.'

'You're trying to hide behind a joke,' Casey said. 'Tell me about him.'

'I don't know anything about him,' I said.

Casey whispered, 'You don't lie very well.'

That remark ended most of our conversation from there to Denver. When the train finally stopped in Union Station, I said goodbye to Casey and Dr Collier Moore. He shook my hand and invited me to visit them if I was ever in Cloud City. I accepted the invitation even though it was only a courtesy. I was certain I would never see them again. And at the time I had no desire to see Casey again.

CHAPTER FIVE

The Denver City marshal's office was near the center of town. After leaving Union Station I found Larimer Street and followed it. On the western horizon I saw the Rocky Mountains, several miles away and shimmering now in the heat of late July.

The marshal's office looked like a fortress. It was constructed of stone blocks, two stories high. The small windows on the second story were barred. I tied Sun King at the tie rail and entered the building through a door that was covered with tin. A young deputy sitting at the front desk looked up at me.

'What do you need, sonny?' he asked.

He could not have been more than a year or two older than I was, but he seemed anxious to put the distance of age and experience between us.

'I want information about the whereabouts of John Fox,' I said.

The deputy laughed in a forced way. He opened a drawer of the desk and brought out a magazine. He folded it open and tossed it across the desk.

'Read that, sonny,' he said.

I realized this was his idea of a joke. The magazine was one that contained fanciful stories of western lawmen and outlaws. This story was about John Fox, calling him 'a desperate desperado who robs trains and stagecoaches and causes mayhem in the state of Colorado.'

'This is a story,' I said. 'I want facts.'

'Just what do you aim to do when you catch up with John Fox?' the deputy asked. 'Bring him in and collect the reward?'

I had not known there was a reward for John Fox's capture. I nodded in reply. The deputy laughed. As he did so, another tin-covered door at the rear of the office opened. A heavy-set man came into the room. On his vest I saw a marshal's badge.

The deputy said loudly, 'We got us another one, Marshal Dobbs.'

'Another what?' the marshal asked.

'Another Fox hunter,' the deputy said, laughing.

The marshal crossed the room and sat on the corner of the deputy's desk. He looked me over. 'You're going after Fox by yourself, are you?'

'Yes, sir,' I said.

The deputy laughed.

'Dry up, Frank,' the marshal said to him.

'I'm looking for information about John

37

Fox's whereabouts,' I said.

Marshal Dobbs picked up a stack of papers and thumbed through them. He pulled one out and handed it to me. It read:

$5,000 REWARD
JOHN FOX
DEAD OR ALIVE

There was no photograph on the poster. At the bottom I read, 'Reward paid by Alexander B. Reston, Denver, Colorado.'

I said, 'I read in the newspaper that John Fox had robbed a stagecoach in the southern part of the state.'

Frank chuckled in a knowing way. 'Fox gets around, don't he?'

Marshal Dobbs ignored his deputy. 'Where are you from, young man?'

'Richmond,' I said. 'I arrived in Denver today, sir.'

'I see,' Marshal Dobbs said. 'Then you likely don't know that John Fox gets the blame for pert' near every holdup between Santa Fe and Miles City. I reckon he pulls his share of them, all right, but the simple truth is, nobody knows where he is.'

'Except Stallcross,' Frank said eagerly.

Marshall Dobbs nodded. 'Stallcross has been on Fox's trail longer than anybody, that's for sure. He's a hound.'

'Who is this man?' I asked.

'He's a detective who works for Mr Reston,' Marshal Dobbs said.

'He'll bring in Fox one day,' Frank said. 'You watch.'

'Maybe,' Marshal Dobbs conceded.

'You can bet Stallcross will do it sooner than a young upstart like this one,' Frank said, gesturing to me.

'Frank,' Marshal Dobbs said irritably, 'you ain't exactly seasoned out yourself. You'd do well to do more listening and less talking.'

The deputy's face grew red as he stared at Dobbs in silent anger. Marshal Dobbs grew uncomfortable and folded his hands together. He said in a mild voice, 'Go get your dinner, Frank.'

Without a word Frank stood, snatched his hat off a peg on the wall, and left the office.

Marshal Dobbs shook his head. 'I reckon he's let this job go to his head. Frank's a nephew of the mayor's. What am I going to do with him?' The question was not directed at me. Dobbs had been thinking aloud. When he discovered it, he shrugged at me and walked back to his own desk.

'What did you say your name was, young man?' he asked.

I had not said. Since Casey had so easily connected my name with John Fox, I had decided to use another. The one that came to mind now was the name of the man who had raised me.

39

'Ben Madison,' I said.

'Ben, I've got a piece of advice for you,' Marshal Dobbs said. 'You might as well give up your idea of tracking down John Fox alone. You're new in these parts. Plenty of seasoned lawmen and bounty hunters have gone after Fox. The ones that got close turned up dead. A healthy young man like you would be better off panning gold in a crick. You'd make your five thousand faster.'

'It's not the money,' I said.

Marshal Dobbs gave me a long look. 'So it's glory you're after.'

I shook my head. I had said too much. But I could not go on and tell him all of it.

'If you've got glory in your eye,' Marshal Dobbs said, 'there ain't no sense in me trying to talk you out of it.'

He was wrong about me, but I had no way of telling him. I turned away and walked to the tin-covered door. Before I went out, I asked if there was a good hotel nearby.

'The Zebulon is down the street on the next corner,' Marshal Dobbs said. 'You'll find a livery across the street.' He added, 'Good luck to you.'

After boarding Sun King in the livery, I took a room in the Zebulon Hotel. It was a four-story red-brick building with stone trim at the corners. I had planned to have supper in the hotel dining room, but I made the mistake of stretching out on the soft bed and closing my

40

eyes. The room was dark when I was awakened by loud knocks on the door. I stumbled out of bed, found the door handle in the darkness, and pulled the door open.

The man in the hallway was distinctive. He was round-shouldered and bull-necked like a fighter. He wore a canvas coat and tan trousers. Above his full upper lip was the fine dark line of a mustache, cropped almost as short as the hair on his bare head.

'Ben Madison?'

I nodded.

'The city marshal told me you'd be in this hotel,' the man said. 'I understand you're hunting John Fox.'

I nodded again. The confusion of being wakened from deep sleep still clouded my mind.

'I've got a proposition you might be interested in,' the man said. 'If you'll let me in, we can talk this over in private.'

I hesitated. I wondered if this man could be trusted. He wore a revolver beneath his canvas coat. Mine was still packed in my saddlebags.

The man might have read my thoughts. 'I know where John Fox is.'

I lit the lamp by the door and let him in. I closed the door behind him and turned to see him looking at my rifle. I had leaned it against the dresser before lying down.

'Can you use that thing?' the man asked.

'Yes, sir,' I said.

41

A smile crossed his face. 'This is the West, Madison. You don't need to call me "sir."' He studied me and went on, 'You look big and strong, but maybe you're a little young for the kind of work I have in mind.'

'What's that?' I asked.

'I've got three men signed on,' he said. 'We're going after Fox. I need more men, but I'm running out of time. Here's the proposition: Sign on, and I'll pay you fifty dollars. If we get Fox, there's another hundred in it for you.'

I said, 'The reward is five thousand dollars.'

'Do you think you're the man to collect it?' he asked.

'I intend to find out,' I said.

'Dobbs said you're a glory hound,' the man said. 'Well, I didn't come here to argue with you. I'm offering you a deal, fair and square. If you want the fifty, sign on. But if you've got a head full of wild ideas, then I won't waste my time on you.'

'Marshal Dobbs told me no one knows where John Fox is,' I said. 'Now you come in here without even giving your name and tell me you know. Why should I believe you?'

My anger brought another quick smile to the man's face. He said, 'I'm Stallcross.'

CHAPTER SIX

Until that moment I had no idea of accepting his offer. Marshal Dobbs had agreed with his deputy that if anybody was likely to catch up with John Fox, it would be Stallcross. I wanted no part in the capture of John Fox. But I realized that an opportunity was here. I could not let it go by.

At my acceptance Stallcross said, 'We leave at midnight, Madison. Bring your own grub. If you don't have a strong horse, get one. We'll do some hard riding tonight.'

Stallcross went to the door and opened it. 'We'll meet up in front of the city marshal's office, midnight sharp. Do you carry a watch?'

'Yes,' I said.

'Be on time,' Stallcross said.

Only after he had gone did I remember that the pocket watch I carried belonged to John Fox.

I went downstairs to the hotel dining room. Along with the meal I ordered two box lunches. Afterward I returned to my room. I rested until half past eleven, then went down to the lobby and turned in my room key to a surprised desk clerk. He must not have seen many guests leave in the middle of the night.

Across the street I paid the liveryman for an extra ration of oats. I led Sun King down the darkened street to the marshal's office in the middle of the block. Four horses were tied at the tie rail there. The front of the office was lighted by lamps hanging on either side of the tin-covered door. The men were bathed in pale lamplight. Stallcross stood at the front edge of the boardwalk, looking down the street first one way, then the other. Two other men leaned against the wall, smoking and talking quietly. One was tall and broad-shouldered. The second man was short and he wore a sombrero and a serape. Stallcross greeted me with a nod.

The door of the marshal's office swung open. Frank came outside. He wore two revolvers and he carried a Winchester.

'Are you ready, Detective Stallcross?' Frank asked.

Stallcross barely glanced at him. 'I'll tell you when, Frank.'

Frank's eyes swept past me, then he turned and walked back inside the office. The tall man who had been leaning against the wall moved close to Stallcross. I overheard him.

'I don't like this. That squirt's an eager beaver.'

'Frank's all right,' Stallcross said. 'He'll do what he's told.'

'You must be hard up to let him tag along,' the tall man said.

'He's sober,' Stallcross said. 'That's the main thing.'

'I don't like eager beavers,' he said. Then he turned to me. 'Who's this one? He's young,

44

too.'

'That's Ben Madison,' Stallcross said. 'Madison, this is Wade Gibson.'

Gibson made no move to shake hands. 'How many more of these babies did you sign, Stallcross?'

Stallcross ignored him for a long moment. 'Two more men. They're late.'

'Probably asleep,' Wade Gibson said. 'We should wait for light.'

'There's no time,' Stallcross said. 'We're pushing it now.'

'Where are we headed?' Gibson asked.

Stallcross did not answer. He looked back at the man who leaned against the wall. His sombrero shadowed his face.

'You ready, Alvarez?'

The man nodded.

Stallcross looked at his watch. My own showed twenty minutes past twelve. Stallcross slapped his hands together and stepped off the boardwalk. He untied his horse's reins.

'Let's ride. Frank!'

Frank came outside, slamming the heavy door behind him. Wade Gibson muttered a protest that we needed more men, but he went to his horse with the rest of us. The night stillness was then filled with the sounds of snorting horses, creaking saddle leather, and jingling spurs. We gathered in a bunch and rode down the street at a fast trot.

We kept the pace outside of Denver, but

45

strung out in a rough line. The road angled south, then cut due west toward the mountains. Straight ahead the front range of the Rocky Mountains cut the starry sky. In little over two hours we entered those mountains, and the air grew cool and fragrant with the smell of pines, and I caught a smell of moisture from a tumbling creek that I heard but never saw.

We trailed Stallcross when he turned off the road and followed the bottom of a canyon. The pace slowed as we rode along a dry riverbed. Here we might have been inside a cave. It was dark as ink. High overhead I saw a few stars, like a narrow crack in the darkness.

Stallcross left the bottom and began the slow ascent up the side of a mountain. Tree branches slapped us, and we strung farther apart. I brought up the rear, following by sound rather than sight.

We dropped down the far side of the mountain. In the valley there the men stopped at a beaver pond and dismounted. The water gleamed dully by starlight.

We watered the horses. Frank complained that he was not a horseman and the ride had rubbed the insides of his legs raw. Wade Gibson suggested that he turn back and go home. Stallcross ended their mounting argument by saying we had more hard riding ahead. He told us all to check our horses to be sure we could make the ride.

We continued up the length of the valley, then crossed a range of mountains. We rode through dense forests of slender pines, and across a high mountain meadow lush with grass. When we stopped again, I was suddenly aware that the sky had turned gray.

We dismounted. Stallcross reached into his saddlebags and brought out several pieces of burlap and lengths of twine. He handed them out to us, four of each.

Frank asked, 'Where the hell are we?'

Stallcross did not answer. 'Tie the burlap on your horses' hoofs. From here on, no talking. No smoking, either. Take off your spurs.'

Wade Gibson said, 'I'm all turned around, Stallcross. Where are we?'

Stallcross smiled. He looked at Alvarez. 'Tell them.'

Alvarez said softly, 'The Roost.'

'The Roost!' Frank exclaimed.

Stallcross said, 'Frank, I want you to keep your voice down.'

'We must be coming in from the south,' Wade Gibson said.

'That's right,' Stallcross said. 'Hell's Gate is just over the next ridge.'

'What's your plan?' Gibson asked.

'Take it,' Stallcross said.

'The Gate?' Gibson asked. 'With whose army?'

'I don't expect it to be guarded,' Stallcross said. 'One guard, at most. We'll take it, all

47

right.'

'Then what?' Gibson asked.

'I'll tell you the rest of it when we get there,' Stallcross said. He looked at Frank, then at me. 'If any of you want to turn back, now's the time to do it.'

No one spoke until Wade Gibson said, 'We're going to be outnumbered. There's no two ways about that.'

'I'm not a man to commit suicide,' Stallcross said. 'We'll take them, Wade.'

'I'm not a-scared,' Frank said.

'Ain't it funny you should be the one to say it,' Gibson said.

'Quit riding me,' Frank said.

'I don't ride jackasses,' Wade Gibson said.

'Save your fighting,' Stallcross said. 'You'll be needing it before this day is out. Are you staying, Madison?'

'I don't know what we're up against,' I said. 'What is this gate you're talking about?'

'You'll understand when we get there,' Stallcross said. 'Hell's Gate is the narrow entrance to the Roost. Whoever commands the Gate has control of the Roost. If it looks sour to you when we get there, you can turn back and ride out the way we came in. That goes for all of you.'

'Hell, I've come this far,' Gibson said. 'Count me in.'

'Me, too,' Frank said, sneering at me.

I nodded at Stallcross.

After we had tied the pieces of burlap on the horses' hoofs, Stallcross said, 'Let's ride, gentlemen. Quietly now.'

We topped the ridge and dropped down the side of a steep-walled canyon. Instead of going to the bottom, Stallcross led us along the side. Despite the steep angle, pine trees grew in abundance.

We stayed close together. At one point the branch of a pine tree snapped back from Stallcross and swatted Frank across the face. He cried out and swore. Stallcross looked back and angrily waved him quiet. I saw Wade Gibson shake his head in disgust.

In the pale sky overhead, thin clouds turned pink and then grew deep red like fire. Stallcross began to drop down the side of the steep ridge. The trees thinned. Far below I saw the canyon bottom, open and grassy. Then ahead I saw Hell's Gate.

The canyon nearly closed at a formation of rocks. In a small opening in these rocks I saw daylight. That was the only way out of the canyon for riders, unless they wanted to take half a day of picking their way up the steep canyon wall.

Stallcross halted. He dismounted and motioned for us to do the same and gather around him. He spoke in a low voice.

'That's the Gate, gentlemen. One man can hold off a hundred up there.'

'Where does that leave us?' Gibson asked.

49

'When John Fox isn't here,' Stallcross said, 'discipline breaks down. I don't expect to find a guard up there.'

'How do you know Fox ain't in the Roost?' Gibson asked.

'We drew him out,' Stallcross said. 'He thinks there's a payroll of Reston's on a northbound stage out of Denver. Alvarez saw Fox lead a dozen men out of here day before yesterday. I look for him to hit the stage this morning. He'll be chased by a posse, but they'll drop off after a few miles. By the time the men get here, they'll think they're in the clear.'

'Until we take them,' Frank said, grinning.

'One thing at a time,' Stallcross said. 'First, we have to have a look at the Gate. Wade, I want you to come with me. No shooting if you can help it. Alvarez, you back us up. Frank, you and Madison stay here with the horses. You can take the burlap off their hoofs now. Lead them up into the trees and tie them good. We want to be sure they can't be seen.'

Though Frank was not happy about being left behind, he did as he was told. We led the horses farther up the steep slope and tied them deep in the pine forest. I used my Bowie knife to cut the twine on all the horses' hoofs. Frank did not help. I saw him open Wade Gibson's saddlebags and plunge his hands down into them. He brought out Gibson's spare canteen. He took a long drink from it, then replaced it.

I pulled my saddlebags off Sun King and sat

down by a tree. I leaned against it. On a branch somewhere above me a bluejay spoke harshly, probably saying I was not welcome. Or he might have been warning me. The next sound I heard was the *click* of a revolver hammer.

I turned and saw Frank aiming one of his revolvers at my face.

'I don't care what Stallcross says,' Frank said, 'you can't back out now. You're in all the way, sonny. Try to run off, and I'll gun you down myself.'

'I believe you would, Frank,' I said, 'if my back was turned.'

Frank was too deep in his thoughts to see the implication of what I said. 'If one of them outlaws seen you, the whole bunch would know something was wrong. You'd get us all killed.'

'Put your gun away,' I said. 'I'm not going anywhere.'

It might have been the first time in his life, but for once Frank was right. No one would be permitted to leave. I had known it ever since we had ridden over the ridge and approached Hell's Gate. Stallcross had only said so to keep us together. He needed his men now, all of us.

Frank somehow had sensed that I would back out if I could. I wondered if Stallcross had read me the same way. Perhaps that was why he had left Frank and me together.

In a quarter of an hour Stallcross, Alvarez, and Wade Gibson returned. They were smiling

51

and talking in normal voices. No guard had been posted in the rocks. Hell's Gate was ours for the taking.

CHAPTER SEVEN

Stallcross sent Wade Gibson and Frank to the far side of the narrow passageway through the rock formation. Then Stallcross pointed to a boulder near the bottom of the rocks and told me to take a position behind it. He and Alvarez stayed above me. Any one of us had full command of the open canyon bottom.

Before settling down behind the boulder, I had looked through the passageway and seen the gently rolling grassland that was known as the 'Roost.' Stallcross told me it was an isolated region generally unknown to outsiders. The Roost was a haven for outlaws. Stallcross mentioned that the lawmen who had gone in there rarely came out in one piece.

Once we were all in position, Stallcross told us not to move around any more than we had to. And he warned us to be prepared for a long wait. He was right. By the middle of the afternoon I had gone through most of my food and water. I was stiff and sore. The others must have been, too, but no one complained. Frank had kept quiet for most of the afternoon. I wondered if he was awake.

52

The sun was low in the sky behind me when I heard Stallcross's urgent whisper: 'Here they come! Here they come!'

Even up to that last moment I had imagined that Stallcross's plan was to wait until the outlaws were close and then we would all jump out from our hiding places like the lawmen in dime novels and command the men to throw down their weapons and surrender. But when I heard the four men scoot into their positions and cock their rifles, I knew I had been living outside reality.

Sweat broke out of me, and tears sprang to my eyes. I brushed my eyes and inched to one side until I could see around the boulder. Ten men rode toward the Gate. They were little more than fifty yards away, strung out in a rough line. One man rode slumped in his saddle as though he was wounded.

As Stallcross had predicted, the men were off their guard. When they drew near the Gate, they bunched. The lead rider took off his hat and waved it over his head. He apparently believed a guard was in the rocks. I wondered if he was John Fox; in the next instant he was punched out of the saddle as rifle shots erupted all around me.

Three other men tumbled out of their saddles and lay sprawled on the ground. A horse squealed and went down. Someone shouted, then screamed. The remaining six riders broke for the cover of the trees. None

53

made it. In a matter of seconds they were cut down. The last man rode a white horse. The animal panicked and reared. I saw his chest blossom red. The horse went over, falling on his rider.

Even after the ten men were down and lay motionless, the shooting went on. Clods of dirt flew up around the bodies. Every time a body was struck by rifle fire, it jerked slightly, as though trying to pull away and retreat from death.

'That's enough!' Stallcross shouted. 'Reload before we move in.'

I stood and immediately became sick. All the food I had eaten that day retched out of me and splattered against the rock that had given me cover—cover from ten men who'd had no chance to defend themselves. My vomiting went on even after there was nothing left, and I was soaked in my sweat.

'Too much for you, Madison?' Wade Gibson said.

I turned, and through my blurred vision saw him looking down at me. Frank leaped over a rock and came to me. He picked up my rifle and felt the barrel.

'Hell, he never even fired. Not once.' The rifle clattered on the rocks at my feet where Frank dropped it.

Stallcross and the others cautiously stepped out into the open. They advanced toward the bodies strewn across the ground, keeping their rifles trained on them. One by one, they turned the bodies over.

With my handkerchief I wiped sweat and tears from my face and walked down to the others. I heard Frank ask which man was John Fox.

'He's not here,' Stallcross said.

Frank shouted, 'He has to be!'

'Fox must have smelled out the trap,' Stallcross said quietly.

I jumped when Alvarez shot two of the wounded horses and put an end to their squealing. The other mounts had run into the trees a short distance and now were looking back at us.

Wade Gibson asked Stallcross if he recognized any of the men. 'Maybe there's reward money out on one.'

Stallcross shook his head tiredly. Then Alvarez found a man who was alive.

Stallcross knelt beside him. The front of the man's chest was bathed in blood that oozed as I looked down at him.

'You're shot to pieces,' Stallcross said. 'Who are you?'

The man's breath rasped slowly through his mouth. I thought he could not speak, but then he said hoarsely, 'Murdering bastards.'

'Who are you?' Stallcross repeated.

'Baxter ... Sam Baxter.'

'Where's Fox?' Stallcross asked.

Sam Baxter coughed weakly. 'You never

55

gave us a chance. We never even seen you.'

'You're damned right, you didn't,' Stallcross said. 'You're dying, Baxter. If you've never told the truth before, you'd better tell it now. Where's John Fox?'

'Go to hell,' Sam Baxter said. 'Every damned one of you.'

'That's where you're headed if you don't tell the truth,' Stallcross said. 'You hit the Reston payroll this morning, didn't you?'

Sam Baxter nodded once. 'What there was of it. Five hundred dollars was all.'

'Fox was leading you, wasn't he?' Stallcross asked.

Sam Baxter moaned. 'Boys, you've killed me, you've killed me.'

'Where's John Fox, Baxter?' Stallcross demanded.

Sam Baxter died as we looked on. He appeared to be staring up at the evening sky, and his last words were: 'Cloud City.' He shook as though chilled, and then he was still.

Stallcross slapped his hands together in a gesture of futility and straightened up. 'Frank, you and Madison go fetch the horses. While you're doing that, we'll try to catch their horses and see if we can find that payroll.'

Frank pointed at me. 'I'm not going anywhere with this coward.'

'Do what I tell you, Frank,' Stallcross said, glancing back toward the Gate. 'This is outlaw country. We don't have time to stand around here arguing.'

Frank turned and ran into the trees toward the horses we had tied. I followed at a slower pace. Frank brought all the horses except mine down the slope. By the time I returned, Alvarez and Wade Gibson had rounded up the horses belonging to the outlaws. In the saddlebags of one, Stallcross found five hundred dollars in currency.

'Fox didn't even take his cut,' Stallcross said.

'How do you figure it?' Wade Gibson asked.

'He must have smelled something sour,' Stallcross said. 'They thought there was a big payroll on the stage. When they didn't find it, Fox must have got suspicious.' Stallcross caught his horse and swung up into the saddle. 'Let's ride, gentlemen.'

Riding fast, we followed the canyon bottom away from Hell's Gate. We made good time by staying in open country. It was barely nightfall when we cut the road that led back to Denver.

I pulled Sun King to a halt. The others rode on, but Stallcross must have missed me, for he came back. He asked if my horse had pulled up lame. I said no, then asked how I could get to Cloud City from here.

'Follow this northbound road and you'll be headed in the right direction,' he said. 'I thought you'd had your fill of manhunting.'

'I've had my fill of your brand of it,' I said.

'There isn't any other kind, Madison,'

57

Stallcross said. 'Take my word for it. You kill them, or they kill you.'

'Then what's the difference between you and them?' I asked.

Stallcross did not answer for a long moment. I could not see the expression on his face, but I heard anger in his voice when he spoke:

'You won't live long, Madison. I can promise you that.' He paused and added in a gentler voice, 'Hell, you might as well ride into Denver and collect your fifty dollars.'

'Keep it,' I said.

'You don't like money?' Stallcross asked. When I did not reply, he said, 'You must want Fox bad to chase after a lead like the one Baxter gave you.'

'He might have been telling the truth,' I said.

'He was a dying man,' Stallcross said. 'He was looking up at the sky and the clouds. That's probably what made him say "Cloud City."'

'I'll find out,' I said.

'I'm thinking you're not after Fox for the reward,' Stallcross said. 'Why are you chasing him?'

'That's between John Fox and me,' I said.

'I thought I liked you, Madison,' Stallcross said. 'Now, I don't know. You got a streak in you that I can't figure.'

I felt more than saw Stallcross's stare. Before he turned his horse and rode away, he said:

'Our trails might cross again, Madison. Be

damned sure you step aside when you see me coming.'

I sat my saddle and listened to the pounding hoofs of Stallcross's horse grow faint. At last I was surrounded by darkness and silence. I needed both. Still very close to my mind's eyes and ears were the sounds of sudden gunfire, squealing horses, and the cries of dying men. My belief that one of them was my father had wrenched me harder than anything I had ever experienced before.

CHAPTER EIGHT

I let Sun King wander along the road at his own pace. I thought I had gone only a short distance when I jerked awake and realized I had nearly fallen out of the saddle. Sun King stopped and looked back at me. I dismounted.

I heard a creek gurgling beside the road. I led Sun King to it. He drank while I rinsed my face. The water was numbing cold. It must have come straight from the snow high in the mountains.

In the darkness I sensed more than saw an open meadow on the other side of the creek. I waded across and led Sun King into high grass. I pulled off his saddle and bridle and hobbled him. I spread the saddle blanket on the ground and lay down on it, resting my head on my saddle.

I woke up squinting against the morning sun. Sun King had wandered into the trees at the edge of the meadow. I took off his hobbles and led him to the creek. While he drank, I ate the last of the two box lunches I had bought at the Zebulon Hotel.

The road led into the foothills. An hour past noon I came to a stage stop and bought a hot meal. I got some supplies—pinto beans, coffee, bacon, and cheese and crackers—and asked for directions to Cloud City. It was three days' ride from here.

The stage stop was located at a fork in the road. The main road cut deep into the mountains. From here on I saw the heavy traffic of stagecoaches, freight wagons with long mule teams, and assorted buckboards and mud wagons. The stagecoaches were piled high with luggage and filled with dusty passengers, mostly men. The smaller wagons carried men, too, with their supplies and mining equipment lashed to the beds. The big freight wagons were loaded with all manner of goods, from canned food to building bricks. All of this traffic was headed for Cloud City, the richest silver camp and wildest boom town of all.

In the high country the air turned cold the instant the sun dipped below the peaks in the afternoons. When I made camp, I'd build up a good fire before turning in. Often I would wake at night, shivering, and I would stoke up the fire with more wood. That way I was assured of finding hot coals in the morning to boil water for coffee and beans.

The road to Cloud City often paralleled a pair of railroad tracks. Once I saw a work train pass by. It was from the Colorado & Western Narrow Gauge Railroad.

On the third day I rode Sun King over a mountain that rose above timberline. The narrow switchback road was jammed with wagon traffic. The crisp air was filled with the curses of teamsters and the popping of whips and the clear jingling of bells on lead animals.

On horseback I made much better time than the slow wagons. Near the top of the mountain the trees were stunted and twisted by the wind. At the very top there was not a tree in sight, and I saw snow.

Down at the bottom of this mountain the traffic strung out. The road was wider here, allowing the faster stagecoaches and light wagons to pass by the big freight wagons.

Sun King pranced and bobbed his head as we heard explosions. Through the trees I saw the work train. Farther ahead I saw a crew working on the roadbed. They were blasting a cut through the granite side of a mountain. By going through a deep canyon, the train avoided the high mountain pass.

Another explosion from the railroad crew made Sun King rear. I dismounted and led him, hoping to calm him. Around a bend in the road I came to a freight wagon that was loaded with red bricks. One wheel had sunk deep into the soft earth beside the road. The freighter was up with his team, trying to urge them ahead. He was getting nowhere.

I led Sun King into the grass beside the road and tied him. I walked over to the freighter and asked if he needed help.

'By God, I do,' he said, grinning to show missing front teeth. He was red-haired and wore a full beard, red, too. 'I don't know who sent you, but you're here at the right time. I'm George Rademacher. Folks call me Red.'

I introduced myself and we shook hands. His grip nearly brought me to my knees. Red walked back to the rear of the wagon, explaining that he had pulled over to the side because his load had shifted. There wasn't much he could do about it, except to tie it again to keep from losing it. When he had tried to pull away, the wheel had sunk.

Red handed me a long, stout pole. He showed me where to slide the pole under the wagon so I could get leverage on the rear axle.

'As soon as you hear me whispering to the team,' Red said, 'put your shoulder under the pole and straighten up.'

'Whisper' was Red's idea of a joke. He took his reins in hand and yelled at the team. I put my weight against the pole and heaved.

The wagon creaked. It inched forward, then fell back. Red hollered and cursed, and the

62

wagon eased forward and at last rolled out of the hole. Red drove several yards ahead to solid ground and halted the animals.

'I've sure got to thank you, Ben,' Red said. 'All the other folks on this road are in too big a hurry to be silver barons to stop and help a man.'

'How much farther is Cloud City?' I asked.

'About ten miles,' Red said. 'You'll come to Stump Town first. That's a mill and smelter town about six, eight miles ahead. Follow the road uphill a couple more miles and you'll be in Cloud City. Do you aim to do some prospecting?'

'No,' I said. 'I'm looking for a man.'

Red's smile faded. 'You ain't the law, are you?'

'No,' I said.

'Well, that's good,' Red said. 'The law don't fare too well in this country. There's twenty thousand men up in Cloud City now. Half of them are starving to death. At night they come into camp looking for a grubstake and a place to sleep. Some ain't too choosy about how they get their stake. If a man looks prosperous, he's likely to get knocked over the head. You might keep that in mind.'

'Thanks, Red, I will,' I said.

The train whistle blew. From where we stood the work engine was out of sight, but Red looked off in that direction.

'Railroad's coming,' he said in a low voice.

'Will it hurt your business?' I asked.

Red snorted as though the answer was obvious. 'There won't be no freighting business when the tracks hit Cloud City.' He added, 'I'm hoping they don't make it this year.'

'What about next year?' I asked.

Red shrugged. 'There'll be another mining camp somewheres, I reckon. Folks will need goods, and I'll haul to them. I can pull this rig anywhere folks need goods.'

I untied Sun King and led him back to the road. 'I'd better be riding,' I said.

Red shook my hand again, hard. 'Ben, you hunt me up in Cloud City tonight and I'll stand you to a dinner. I'll be in the Rocky Mountain Boys' Saloon. If I ain't there, I'll be in the Taylor House dining room.'

'I'll do that, Red,' I said.

'So long, Ben,' he said.

In little over an hour's ride the road led into a small basin that held Stump Town. It was well named. The surrounding hillsides were covered with tree stumps. I saw why. The shacks and tents of town were built around two smelters. These were long, windowless structures with tall chimneys. The brick chimneys belched great clouds of yellow-green smoke. Around the smelters I saw large piles of black waste. Among these piles were charcoal ovens. They had consumed the forest.

One smelter looked new. As I rode closer, I

saw the name RESTON painted on the roof in capital letters.

Everything and everyone in Stump Town was covered with soot. The air was foul with fumes. I followed the road that wound randomly through Stump Town and saw that several of the larger tents and log buildings had crude signs nailed above their doors, announcing themselves to be hotels, cafes, or mercantiles. Many were saloons. One canvas-roofed log saloon was simply named: Stump.

Out of the basin, the road switchbacked up a steep hillside. Traffic was heavy here, and dangerous. Ore wagons lurched down the road at breakneck speed, apparently ready to run down anyone who was in the way.

From higher ground I looked back at Stump Town. Blanketed by the yellowish cloud and coated with soot, it looked like a soiled hole in the earth.

Ahead, I heard Cloud City before I saw the camp. Gunshots were the first sounds I heard. Then I topped the hillside and rode out onto a flat, ringed by mountains. As I drew nearer, I heard shouts of men and squeals of women and music from a brass band.

Cloud City sprawled across the flat, ten thousand feet in altitude, all the way up the sides of the surrounding mountains. On these mountains were hundreds of mines. Some were small, others very large. Below the tunnels and shafts were piles of earth that had been carried or hauled out. The piles were yellow and brown, as though the earth, when opened, had bled these colors.

The road led straight into Cloud City's main thoroughfare, Carbonate Street. This narrow street, paved with slag from the smelters, was lined with brick and stone buildings, and many frame buildings, all unpainted.

On side streets that led away from Carbonate, I saw a confusion of tents and log cabins and living quarters that were little more than several boards knocked together and partially covered with canvas. Among these were a few elegant homes, colorfully painted and decorated with gingerbread trim. All of them, from shacks to mansions, were jammed close together. Land must have been sold by the square inch in Cloud City.

A brass band played in front of a dance hall on Carbonate. As I rode past the buildings on this street, I noticed that many of them were gambling houses and saloons and dance halls. Few were business buildings. On a corner was the Taylor bank. Next door was the Taylor House, and next to it was the Rocky Mountain Boys' Saloon.

I rode Sun King to the far end of town. A sawmill was here, with piles of logs on one side and stacks of cut lumber on the other. I turned Sun King back. On a side street I had seen a sign that pointed to a livery stable on one of the unnamed side streets.

66

Miners crowded the boardwalks. Many were drunk and tried to push others off the walk into the street. Some attempted to sing with the brass band. I saw few women. Most of them were dance hall girls, overdressed in their outrageous hats of plumed feathers and cheap jewelry. I looked at each one of them as I rode along Carbonate Street. I surprised myself when I realized I was watching for Casey.

CHAPTER NINE

After boarding Sun King, I followed the narrow side street back to Carbonate Street. The late-afternoon sky had become clouded, and a cold wind was picking up. My cotton coat was too light for this country. On Carbonate Street I found a clothing store. A sheepskin coat was displayed in the window.

I told the clerk in the store that I wanted a coat like the one in the window. He took me to a rack of them, and I tried several on until I found one that fit. The twenty-five-dollar price was twice what I expected to pay, but I doubted that I would find a cheaper one in Cloud City.

Outside I wore the new coat and carried my old one. At this hour there was little traffic on Carbonate Street. I crossed it without endangering my life and went into the dining room that adjoined the Taylor House. Well-dressed men and their ladies sat at the tables. As I was shown to a table, I wondered why a freighter like Red would come here. He did not strike me as the kind of man who would want to be seen with businessmen and dandies.

The menu offered venison and elk steaks and bear meat 'when available.' I ordered elk steak. When it arrived, I knew why a big man like Red came here to eat. The steak was two inches thick and nearly as big as the platter it was served on. The waiter brought side dishes of vegetables and then a large slice of apple pie. The meal was very expensive—three dollars and fifty cents—but all the food was delicious, and there was plenty of it.

I left the Taylor House without seeing Red. I took an evening walk along the boardwalk. It was fast growing dark. The brass band still played in front of the dance hall. A gambling house next door displayed a dozen kerosene lamps in a row, and a barker stood outside the door, loudly encouraging men to come in and get rich at the tables.

I walked to the Cloud City Hotel. I went in and asked for a room. The desk clerk looked at me as though I had dropped in from another planet. The Cloud City Hotel was filled, the clerk told me, and had been since the day it opened. The waiting list was as thick as the Bible.

I left the hotel, crossed the street, and walked along that boardwalk. It was full dark now and very cold. The wind drove the miners and smelter workers into the gambling houses and saloons. The band had retreated into the dance hall. The only music outside now was played by the mountain wind.

I began noticing that many men were huddled in doorways. Most wore tattered clothes. Some had no coats at all, but wore a thin blanket or even pieces of canvas wrapped around them.

One such man stopped me on the boardwalk. Through chattering teeth he asked me to stake him. He knew the location of a rich silver deposit, and all he needed was money to buy tools and food. Half the silver he found would be mine, he said. I told him I had no money to invest. I gave him my cloth coat. When I left him, he was digging through the pockets, looking for a stray coin or some tobacco, I guessed.

I passed in front of the gambling house that had a row of kerosene lamps burning in front. The cold must have driven the barker inside, too. I peered through the window and saw a large, smoky room crowded with men of all descriptions. Some looked no better than those huddled together on the street; others were immaculately dressed and appeared wealthy. Show girls mingled with them.

At the far end of this room, past the gaming tables and roulette wheels, there were half a dozen dancing girls on a stage. To one side of them a sign read: 'See the blonde KIT KAT do her DARING ACT!'

I walked on, watching for another hotel. As I passed the darkened store where I had bought the sheepskin coat, a man leaped out of the shadows and grasped my arm.

I was startled and tried to pull away. The man held on tightly. He was old and wore ragged clothes. His long, gray beard and hair were tangled.

'Listen, youngster, I've got legal claim to diggings that'll run a thousand dollars to the ton, maybe more. You stake me, and you'll be a rich child tomorrow. A few dollars is all I ask.'

I told him no and again tried to pull away from his grasp. For an old man, he was strong. He held on as though his life depended on me.

'What goes on here?'

The old miner suddenly let loose. The man who had spoken moved between us. He wore a dark suit and a straight-brimmed hat.

'Ain't nothing going on,' the miner said. 'Me and this youngster was just a-talking.'

'That isn't the way I heard it,' the man said. 'I believe you wanted a stake from this young man and wouldn't take no for an answer.'

The old miner muttered under his breath.

'Be on your way,' the man said. After the old miner had moved down the boardwalk, the man turned to me. 'There are desperate men in this camp, young man. You must be wary

70

about walking around here after dark. I happened to see you in the lobby of the Cloud City Hotel. Have you found a place to stay for the night?'

'Not yet,' I said.

'I thought not,' the man said. 'All the hotels will be filled by now. There is a boardinghouse farther down the way here that you can probably get into at this hour. Come along with me and I'll point you in the right direction.'

'Thank you,' I said. I was grateful to this man, but I could not get a good look at him. The flat brim of his hat kept the light from his face. As we walked along the boardwalk away from the lights of Cloud City, I became more aware of his voice than his appearance. He spoke like an educated man.

We passed the side street that led to the livery stable and walked on to the next.

'Hike up this street about fifty, sixty yards, young man,' he said. 'You'll see the boardinghouse up there. It's on the left-hand side of the street.'

The 'street' was little more than a narrow alley between two false-fronted buildings. It was dark. I turned to thank the man for helping me, but he had already moved away and was walking back the way we had come.

My boots sunk into half-frozen mud as I walked up the side street. I had gone only a dozen paces when I heard someone running

71

toward me from behind. Before I could turn around, I heard the voice of the man who had just left me:

'I'm sorry. My God, I'm sorry!'

Something hard slammed against the side of my head. Sparkling flashes of light erupted inside my eyes.

I felt cold mud against the side of my face. I sat up. My sheepskin coat had been opened and my shirt was torn. The money belt was gone. When I stood, I staggered and fell against the wall of one of the buildings. I rested there until my head cleared.

I reached to my hip pocket and felt my wallet. But it wasn't until I made my way back to Carbonate Street and reached into my front trouser pockets that I realized the gold pocket watch was gone.

I thought I had been unconscious only a few minutes. The noise of music and merriment two blocks away was as loud as ever. I wiped mud from my face and walked in that direction. I remembered seeing the marshal's office on the same side street that led to the livery stable.

The Cloud City marshal was in the office, talking to a prisoner. Four cells were at the rear of the log building. The marshal turned and watched me enter.

'Don't tell me,' he said. 'Some bastard knocked you over the head and stoled your money.'

72

'That's right,' I said.

'And you're plenty mad,' he said.

I nodded.

'Well, what's your name?' the marshal asked as he crossed the room to his desk.

'Ben Madison,' I said.

He wrote my name in a book. Without looking up, he asked, 'What did he look like?'

'I didn't get a good look at him, Marshal—' I paused.

'Coe,' he said. 'The name's Coe.'

'The man was about my height,' I went on. 'He was slender. He wore a dark suit and a straight-brimmed hat.'

One of the prisoners laughed.

Marshal Coe said, 'That description fits a few thousand men. Would you know him if you saw him again?'

'I might,' I said. 'I'm sure I'd recognize his voice. He was well-spoken like an educated man.'

The prisoner laughed again.

Marshal Coe said over his shoulder, 'Shut up, Shorty.' To me, he asked, 'What did you lose?'

'A gold watch and my money belt,' I said.

'How much money was in the belt?'

'About seven hundred dollars,' I said.

'You'll never see it again,' Marshal Coe said casually. 'What did the gold watch look like?'

I described it to him by the engraving on the cover and the photograph inside.

73

'Well, the watch might turn up,' Marshal Coe said. 'I'll keep an eye out for it. Check back with me.'

'Aren't you going to do anything?' I realized I had shouted.

'Now, you calm down, young man,' Marshal Coe said, pointing his pencil at me. 'Cloud City is the biggest damned boom town this state has ever seen. I've got three deputies for this whole camp. We have our hands full every night with shootings. There's hardly a night goes by without a killing. You're lucky you only got slugged. And you're damned lucky you're still wearing boots and a good coat. I've seen young men like you come in here picked clean.'

I was angered by his attitude of futility, but I knew nothing would be gained by shouting at him.

'I'll find him,' I said.

Marshal Coe nodded. 'Well, maybe you will. But if you kill him, you'll find yourself in my jail. That's a promise.'

The prisoner named Shorty laughed again. I turned away and walked to the door. My eye was caught by a 'Wanted' poster on the bulletin board. The poster was a copy of the one I had seen in Denver that offered a five-thousand-dollar reward for John Fox.

Outside I stood on the boardwalk at the corner by the marshal's office and Carbonate. I buttoned my coat against the icy wind and

74

jammed my hands into the pockets. I was ashamed and angry with myself. The man who robbed me had led me to that darkened alley like a lamb to slaughter. Now all the money I had to my name was what was left in my wallet—less than five dollars.

Judge Madison had been right. I had led a sheltered life for seventeen years, and I was unable to survive on my own.

Yet I had no choice. I must survive. I walked back up the side street to the livery where I had boarded Sun King. I asked the liveryman if I could sleep there tonight. He said no and recited a long speech about how if he let me sleep there, he could not turn others away and sooner or later he would have a boardinghouse instead of a livery and in time somebody would likely fall asleep while smoking and he would be burned out.

I wished I had never asked. I inquired where a boardinghouse was. Farther up the street, he said, I would find several.

I followed the street up the hillside. The first frame boardinghouse I came to had a sign over the door saying the place was filled. I walked on, keeping my hand on my revolver. I had no intention of being taken by surprise again. Somewhere I had read that any man could make a mistake, but the man who made the same mistake twice was a fool.

I found a low log building with a lamp lighted over the door. The sign read

'Morgan's 25¢.'

A burly man answered my knock. He blocked the doorway and held out his hand. 'Twenty-five cents.'

He stepped aside when I handed him a quarter. The inside of the log building was lit only by a lamp with a smoked chimney. The burly man tossed me a light blanket and pointed into the gloom. On the floor I saw many rounded shapes of sleeping men.

'Squeeze up tight,' the burly man said. He added, 'Keep your boots on, or you'll lose 'em.'

As I made my way into the room, I saw bunks along the wall. The men who came in earliest got them, I guessed. Everyone else slept on the floor.

I lay down on the floor amid the sounds of snoring men. I pulled the blanket around me, but quickly pushed it away because of its smell. The man who slept to one side of me wheezed loudly as though sick. It was very cold, yet because of all the men in the room, the air was close and stinking.

During the night the door opened several times, admitting others who paid their quarters and stretched out on the floor. One was a young man who was well dressed. He assured the burly man he would not be here at all if he had not been knocked out and robbed in a brothel. The burly man was unimpressed and would not let him in until he paid his quarter like the others. I found some small comfort in

76

the young man's misery. I was not alone.

The sounds of men tramping out of Morgan's woke me. I sat up and blinked against the daylight that streamed in through the open front door. The burly man stood there, watching the men leave in as stern a way as he had watched them enter.

I stood and looked down at the man who had wheezed most of the night. He was quiet now, and I thought he had finally been able to sleep.

The burly man crossed the room and looked at the man, too. He nudged him with his toe. Then he stooped and pulled the blanket off him. As soon as I saw the man's white face, I knew he was dead. The burly man swore.

'You know him?' he asked me.

'No,' I said.

'He never should have come in here,' the burly man said. 'I knowed he was sick. He never should have come in here.'

I felt my face grow warm with anger. 'What did you want him to do—stay outside?'

The burly man seemed not to hear me. 'Now I'm stuck with another dead one.'

I hurried out of Morgan's, away from the stench and away from the burly man, who was ice cold himself. I walked down the hill toward Carbonate Street. Other men were moving in the same direction, yawning and slapping themselves. Rivulets of water that coursed down the hillside were frozen solid now.

I counted my money and found the same four dollars and few coins that I had known were there. I walked past the Taylor House dining room and smelled breakfast cooking. I passed a bakery and smelled fresh bread.

One of the last buildings on Carbonate Street, down by the sawmill, was a log structure that served greasy food all day and most of the night. Yesterday I had ridden past on Sun King, knowing I would never eat in a place like this. Today I went inside.

The walls were covered with cheap muslin. There were long benches on either side of the plank tables. The smell of something burned and the smell of rancid grease filled the room as I took a place with the crowd of men on the benches. I bought two cold biscuits and a cup of weak coffee for twenty-five cents. Grease swam on top of the coffee.

By sunup Carbonate Street had filled with traffic. Businessmen swept off the boardwalk in front of their stores. The gambling houses and dance halls were locked up and dark behind their windows. They would be open at ten in the morning.

I crossed the street and walked to the sawmill. Over the screams of the steam-powered saws, I asked the foreman for a job. He said he had a full crew. In the camp I asked a dozen proprietors of various shops for work, but none of them were hiring. There might have been a hundred men for every job in

78

camp.

By midday I was doing what many other men were doing: I leaned against a building and watched the traffic go by on Carbonate. In the afternoon I went into the Rocky Mountain Boys' Saloon. I drank a nickel mug of beer and looked around for the freighter named Red. His offer to buy my supper looked better than ever now.

After a while the bartender noticed I was not doing much damage to the beer. He told me to drink up or move on. This wasn't a hotel, he said. I finished the beer and left without finding Red.

That evening I paid fifty cents to get into the boardinghouse that was below Morgan's. I expected the boardinghouse to be much better, but it wasn't. The two-story building was divided into small rooms. The rooms were crowded with beds. They were unclean and stank.

The next day I stood idle on the street. My hunger made me dizzy and made me feel aimless. At noon I went into one of the better cafes and bought a good meal. It cost a dollar, but filled me. I came outside with an idea.

The man who had robbed me said he had seen me in the lobby of the Cloud City Hotel. Perhaps if I went there, I would see him. I walked into the carpeted lobby of the hotel and was met by a doorman. He wore a dark uniform and a cap with a pink ribbon around it. He told me I did not look like the kind of man who had any business in the Cloud City Hotel.

Until then I did not realize how miserable I looked. The first time I had come in, I had looked presentable. Now I was unshaven and needed a bath. There was still dried mud on my clothes.

The doorman's abrupt manner brought my anger and frustration to the surface. We exchanged hot words, and when I raised my fist, a woman screamed. Bellhops joined the doorman and took my arms and shoved me toward the door.

I pulled my right arm free and managed to hit one of the bellhops and knock his cap off, but the others pitched me out the door. I rolled into the street.

I got to my knees and thought of going back in to settle the score. Men and women on the boardwalk were staring at me. Among them was a young woman who turned away from me and hurried into the hotel lobby. I knew I had seen her before, but several moments passed before I realized she was Casey.

CHAPTER TEN

I hurried away from the Cloud City Hotel. My surprise at seeing Casey was replaced by a

80

sudden determination to leave camp. I would ride back over the mountains to civilization and find work. After I had saved some money I could return.

The plan no sooner came to mind when I heard a shout. I looked across the street and saw Red. He waved and ran across Carbonate Street. We shook hands, and he clapped me on the back and said he had been looking all over hell for me.

'From appearances, I'd say you've come on hard times, Ben,' Red said. 'Come into this cafe here and I'll stand you to supper.'

The cafe was one of the best in camp and was almost as expensive as the Taylor House. Red was in a cheerful mood and told me he had sold his bricks for the highest price yet: eighty dollars per thousand.

Red fell silent. 'What happened to you, Ben? Did you ever locate the man you was hunting?'

'No,' I said. I told him what had happened the first evening I was in camp. 'You warned me, Red. I should have been more careful.'

'I never warned you about slick operators who put on airs of being your friend,' Red said. 'That's the lowest varmint on earth. Did you get a look at him?'

'It was too dark,' I said. 'He chose his spot.'

'What do you aim to do now, Ben?' Red asked.

'I'll have to leave Cloud City,' I said. 'I need to find work, and there isn't any here. When I get some money saved, I'll be back.'

'What's your trade?' Red asked.

'I don't have one,' I said.

'You don't have a trade?' Red asked. 'What have you done all your life?'

'I went to school,' I said.

Red scowled. 'No offense, Ben, but what the hell good is an education if you don't learn something that'll keep you from starving to death?'

At that moment the question was a good one. I had no answer for it.

When Red finished eating, he pushed his plate aside and moved the white porcelain coffee cup in front of him.

'You still have your rifle and that good-looking horse, don't you, Ben?'

I nodded.

'I've got an idea,' Red said. 'You interested?'

I nodded again. 'Let's hear it.'

'I'm remembering the first trip I made to this camp,' he said. 'I was hauling bricks then, too. Taylor had just finished building his bank. For a spell there wasn't a market for building bricks. So here I sat with a load I couldn't sell. I knew I could sooner or later, but it costs money to sit around here. When I was down to my last silver dollar, I went into a gambling hall and wagered it on the roulette wheel.' He paused. 'And I lost it. I haven't gambled since. You ain't got a weakness for gambling, have you?'

'I don't know,' I said.

82

'Well, I reckon you'll find out one day,' Red said. 'Anyhow, I've learned that when a man is broke is the time he gets his best ideas. All I had been doing before was lounging around camp, feeling sorry for myself.'

'That's what I was doing,' I said.

'You and a few thousand others,' Red said. 'Well, my idea was this: I took my rifle and a couple mules off my rig, and I hiked up into the hills and brought down meat.'

'You hunted?' I asked.

Red nodded. 'The mountains above here is full of deer and elk. Bear, too. I'd shoot them, field dress them, and quarter them. Then I'd bring the meat down to Slaughterhouse Gulch. The slaughterhouse will buy every bit of fresh meat you can carry to them. Have you ever hunted?'

'Only small game,' I said.

'Well, I'll get you started,' Red said. 'You helped me when I needed help. Now I'll give you a hand.'

I started to thank him, but he raised his hands. 'Don't be too quick to thank me. You'll find the work hard—and lonely.'

We went to the livery, where Red picked out two good mules. He haggled with the liveryman for half an hour until the price was down to where he thought it should be. I offered to throw in the last of my money to help pay for the animals, but Red would have none of it. He insisted on buying the two mules and

83

loaning them to me.

Red rented a saddle horse, then he showed me how to tie the mules so one would follow the other. We rode up the hill into a mining district known as Stray Horse Gulch. I saw hundreds of silver mines. Some were little more than holes in the ground, worked by one man with a pick and shovel and wheelbarrow. Others were larger, surrounded by huge piles of earth and rock that had been brought out of tunnels and shafts. The sounds of puffing steam engines were common in Stray Horse Gulch. The engines operated heavy cables that pulled ore buckets out of the earth.

While riding through the mining district Red told me several stories of men who became wealthy from silver in the Cloud City region. I had heard snatches of some of these stories while I had been in camp. One concerned the man named Taylor, who owned the bank and the Taylor House and was the current mayor of Cloud City.

When the Cloud City silver strike was new, Walter Hayes Taylor came as a shopkeeper. His wife turned their home into a small boardinghouse. Between them they made a meager living. Walter Hayes Taylor had done as much prospecting as his spare time would allow—and as much as his domineering wife would allow—but had never found much ore. It was generally agreed that Taylor never did have much idea of what to look for.

84

Against his conservative wife's relentless advice, Walter Hayes Taylor often grubstaked prospectors. The grubstakes consisted of a few tools and some food from his store. This practice was done behind his wife's back as much as possible and brought Taylor no return until the day he staked two Hungarian cobblers. This pair had a wide reputation for using the small amounts of ore they found to buy whiskey. The whiskey consumed, the cobblers would find someone to grubstake them and return to the mountains to prospect. When Taylor's wife learned that her husband had grubstaked these two men, she threatened to leave him. But she did not make good her threat, and the next week the Hungarians returned. Both were roaring drunk. They had found some silver near the surface of the ground. Taylor's wife ran the two men off. Later Walter Hayes Taylor met with them secretly and bought their claim for two hundred dollars. The Hungarians went directly to the Cloud City camp to put the money to proper use. By dumb luck, Walter Hayes Taylor had struck it rich.

Red pointed out the Taylor Mine as we rode past. Red said the last he had heard, the mine was producing silver worth thirty thousand dollars per month. In the first year of the mine's operation, it produced twice that amount.

Over his wife's objections, Taylor reinvested his money and bought other mines. One mine was called the Tip Top. Taylor paid a handsome price for the mine on the basis of ore samples. These were later discovered to have been stolen from the original Taylor Mine. Everyone except Walter Hayes Taylor had known it all along. The Tip Top, besides being full of water now, had never been a good mine. Taylor shrugged off this costly practical joke, pumped the water out of the Tip Top, and began operation. Within a month he struck ore. The strike was a rich one. The Tip Top mine began paying almost as well as the Taylor Mine.

The man could do no wrong. Walter Hayes Taylor was sought out by men from all parts of the country who asked his advice on mining. Walter Hayes Taylor was the richest man in the state of Colorado. Though he had gained no great knowledge, he was listened to.

Red led the way up Stray Horse Gulch and beyond the mining district. We rode through patches of snow over a high mountain that Red identified as Snowshoe Mountain. We dropped into the valley below the summit. In this land untouched by miners there was clear water, open meadows heavy with high mountain grasses, and hillsides forested with pines and aspen trees. Near the stream in the valley we found deer and elk tracks. In the mud we saw clawed tracks that had been left by a bear that morning.

We caught up with the elk herd. Thirty of the

86

big animals grazed along the tree line by an open meadow. We dismounted and slowly crawled toward them. A few of the bulls regarded us casually, then went back to their grazing.

Red and I were less than fifty yards away from the herd when several of the bulls and cows began to fidget and sniff the air. Red stopped crawling and whispered to me.

'See that cow that's sniffing the air?' Red asked. 'On the count of three, shoot her. Hit her just behind her shoulder, and she'll drop in her tracks.'

On Red's whispered count of three, we both fired. The herd bolted and ran into the trees. Two cows were left behind.

'That's good shooting, Ben,' Red said.

That day Red taught me how to field dress and quarter the elk, then he showed me how to secure the meat to the pack saddles on the mules. This was the hard work Red had warned me about. A quarter of a field-dressed elk was heavy. It was suppertime by the time we rode back over Snowshoe Mountain.

Slaughterhouse Gulch was the mining district next to the Stray Horse district. We followed the winding ore wagon road down the steep gulch to the slaughterhouse. It was a large frame building with no windows. Through an open door I saw fresh meat hanging on big steel hooks.

As Red had predicted, the owner of the

slaughterhouse was glad to see us. He was a bald man who wore a stained white apron. He inspected the meat, nodding approvingly. Red had told me there was one slaughterhouse for the whole camp. The butchers worked eighteen hours a day to keep up with the demand.

We sold the two quartered elk for fourteen dollars. Red handed the money to me. I tried to split it with him, but he would not accept his share.

'That's your stake, Ben,' Red said. 'See what you can do with it.'

We ate supper at the Taylor House. Afterward Red told me he was leaving in the morning. He wanted to haul another load of brick over the mountains before the snow fell. Winter came early here. We shook hands and promised to meet again in the Rocky Mountain Boys' Saloon.

When Red wanted to get an early start in the morning, he slept in his wagon. That kept him from getting spoiled, he said. As I watched him walk away that evening, I felt a deep sense of gratitude toward him. He had helped me more than I could ever repay him. I had never felt the same about Judge Madison.

I bought a bath and a haircut and stayed in a two-dollar rooming house that night. I got out of my clothes and slept in a clean bed. Early the next morning I saddled Sun King at the livery stable, tied my pack mules in a string, and rode away from the camp on the road up Stray

Horse Gulch.

I hunted all day without finding the herd of elk. In the afternoon I shot a buck deer. I field dressed him and quartered him. In the evening I rode to the slaughterhouse. I was paid four dollars for my day's work.

That night I did some figuring and found that if I made four dollars every day I would just about break even after paying for my room, meals, and keep for Sun King and the pack mules. I resolved to start looking for another place to live. Even if I had to build a crude lean-to in the mountains, I would be better off than trying to live in the Cloud City camp.

In the morning I bought enough supplies to keep me going for a few days. As long as the weather was fair, I planned to stay in the mountains.

I left the general mercantile and heard a man call my name. I turned to see Dr Collier Moore.

'Well, Benjamin, it's a pleasure to see you,' he said. 'What are you doing in this mountain paradise?'

'Trying to stay alive like everybody else,' I said. 'How are you?'

'Fine, just fine,' Dr Collier Moore said. 'I have an office over the Taylor bank. You must come and see me. Casey would like to see you, too, I'm sure.'

I wasn't. I was certain she had recognized me when I had been thrown out of the Cloud City

89

Hotel. Apparently she had not mentioned that incident to her father.

Dr Collier Moore invited me to supper that evening. I told him I was on my way out of camp, and was glad I had an armload of supplies to prove it. I liked Dr Collier Moore, but I imagined spending an uncomfortable evening with Casey. I promised to look him up in a week or so.

Before we parted, Dr Collier Moore was joined by a chunky, bearded man whom I had seen pointed out by loungers on the boardwalks. He was Walter Hayes Taylor. He and Dr Collier Moore appeared to have become fast friends.

CHAPTER ELEVEN

In the following days I became a better hunter. I learned to track the animals and to look for fresh sign. If I did not find elk by midday, I would hunt deer. Deer were more plentiful and easier to find. I could always down two, and often I got three or four.

During the second week I ranged farther away from Snowshoe Mountain in search of an elk herd. I found them. And I found a cabin.

The old cabin was in a small valley, barely out of sight of the summit of Snowshoe Mountain. Built of thick logs, the cabin was less than five feet high, doorless and windowless, and most of the roof was caved in.

On first sight I knew that this was what I was looking for. There was good grass in the small valley. A narrow but deep stream gurgled along the edge of the grassy meadow. The cabin was several miles away from the mining districts, yet within easy riding distance of Cloud City.

I returned to Cloud City and sold the day's kill to the slaughterhouse. At the sawmill I bought enough scraps of lumber to make a door. I stopped at a hardware store in Cloud City and bought a few tools—a hammer, a saw, an ax, and a handful of nails. After buying canned goods, I hurried back to the cabin.

I spent the next day working on the door of the cabin and the roof. The roof was the hardest. I felled several small pine trees, cut off the branches, and laid them across the top logs. Then I wove branches and boughs in between. It was crude, but the roof would shed some weather. When the heavy snows came, I planned to be gone.

I used the cabin as a headquarters. I had discovered that there were three herds of elk in the region surrounding Snowshoe Mountain, and now I began seeing a pattern to their movements. I understood why Red had been able to ride directly to one of the elk herds.

I saw a few other hunters in the mountains. I stayed clear of them, as they did of me. They all appeared to be loners, and that suited me. Even though two hunters would bring in more meat than one, I had no desire to take on a partner.

Red had been right when he told me that hunting for the slaughterhouse could be a fast way to make money. I had asked him why more men did not become hunters. Red answered by saying that men usually stay with the work they know. The mill workers and smelter men had worked in mills and smelters somewhere else. So had many of the miners. Even the miners who were inexperienced stayed close to the big silver strikes. The men were here to get rich, not to provide meat for the camp.

For the first time in my life I was truly alone. The nights were calm and peaceful, with only the sounds from Sun King or the mules or the far away cries of coyotes to provide company. At dawn I would leave the cabin, hunt for most of the day, carry fresh meat to the slaughterhouse, then return to the cabin by nightfall. I slept on a bed of pine boughs, and my saddle was my pillow.

As my hunting skills sharpened, I bought a third mule. Then my earnings were increased by a third every time all the pack animals were loaded from the day's hunt. And there were few days when I did not load all of them. I could usually predict where the elk herds would travel from one day to the next, and it was always exciting to ride over a ridge and find elk exactly where I thought they would be.

The work was hard. I grew stronger, and my sore muscles disappeared. I did not shave or cut my hair. My clothes became seasoned from the blood of animals and from grass and mud after the many times I crawled after my prey. Judge Madison would not have approved of my condition. He had raised me to be a gentleman.

When I stopped in Cloud City to buy a loaf of bread from the bakery or a box full of canned goods from the general mercantile, I would buy a copy of the camp's newspaper, the *Chronicle*. Back at the cabin I would read the paper by lamplight, looking for mention of John Fox. I found none.

One afternoon when I was in Cloud City, I saw Casey. I was inside the bakery. I watched her pass by on the boardwalk only a few feet away. She did not see me. Casey was dressed in white, wearing white gloves, a long white dress with puffed sleeves, and her blond hair was tied with a wide white ribbon. She held the arm of her companion, a chunky, bearded man wearing a dark suit and a diamond-studded watch fob that sparkled even from a distance. I recognized the man. He was Walter Hayes Taylor.

In the high mountains above Cloud City I saw the season pass. Aspen leaves turned from summer's pale green to autumn's bright yellow and then to gold, all within the space of three

93

weeks. The gold leaves were brittle. With the smallest gust of wind, they clattered delicately. And soon the leaves began to fall as the air turned colder and the winds grew bitter. On the earth the gold leaves curled and turned the color of rust.

Though I remained alone in those weeks, I never became lonely or despairing. My mind sifted through the memories of my past. I looked back on my life and did not like what I saw. Judge Madison had been right when he said I had lived a sheltered life. But I remembered he had suggested I could not survive 'out there.' He was wrong about that. I was not only surviving, I was growing stronger as the work toughened me. There were new challenges every day, and I woke before dawn each morning eager to face them.

The one challenge I dreaded was going to Cloud City. The camp had a foul smell. Some of it drifted up from Stump Town, but most of the stench was from thousands of men living close together. Rotting odors of their garbage and their leavings filled the air and cast a rank, invisible cloud over Cloud City.

I was always glad to return to my cabin after delivering meat to the slaughterhouse. I kept a clean camp. And I loved the smells there. The pine-smelling wind often whispered through the forest. And smoke from my cookfire carried the scent of pine sap.

The *Chronicle* not only gave me something

to read, but the paper also started my cookfires in the mornings and evenings. One evening as I built a teepee of twigs over the wadded newspaper and touched a match to it, the paper leaped to flames and opened slightly. As I watched, the date on top of the newspaper appeared for an instant before being consumed. I realized with a shock that it was the date of my eighteenth birthday. Yesterday or the day before I had turned eighteen, an event I had looked forward to for several years. Now it had passed, unnoticed by me and suddenly consumed by fire and by time.

Several days later I was in camp buying supplies when I heard a shout.

'Ben!'

I turned around and saw Red. He waved his hat over his head and ran across the street toward me, his red hair and beard flowing behind.

'Look at you!' Red shouted. He slapped me across the back, hard. 'You look like a damned wild hunter!'

We went to the Rocky Mountain Boys' Saloon. I hardly recognized my own reflection in the big mirror behind the bar. My hair was long and tangled, and the lower part of my face was covered with a scraggly beard. The skin that showed on my face was the color of tanned hide.

Red invited me to have supper with him at the Taylor House. Before meeting him there, I went to a barbershop and got the full treatment: a shave and a haircut and steaming hot bath.

During supper Red remarked that the steaks we were eating might well have come from animals I had brought out of the mountains. I told Red about my cabin and that I had bought another mule.

'I'm proud of you, Ben,' he said.

I told him I could not have done it without his help.

'Maybe so,' Red said. 'But you've done a heap of work on your own. Nobody's done that for you.'

Red went on to tell me that he had had no trouble in selling his load of bricks. If the price went up any higher, he said, he might as well be hauling silver bricks. Red noted the weather had been unusually fair. He thought he could haul one more load before the snows came. The mountain pass would be blocked to wagon traffic then.

'This'll be my last season in these parts,' Red said. 'The train crews are within spitting distance of Stump Town. Even if they don't get no fu'ther before winter hits this country, a freighter like me will be out of the picture.'

'Why don't you throw in with me?' I asked. 'The two of us could bring down plenty of meat.'

Red grinned but shook his head. 'I'm a freighter, Ben. I only do other work when I got

96

no choice.'

'You could haul ore out of the mines,' I said.

Red pretended to take offense. 'I said I was a freighter, Ben, not no rock hauler.' He added, 'Hell, the railroad will get here sooner or later, no matter what. I'll just have to hunt up another mining camp somewheres. Something always seems to come up about the time I've spent my last dollar.'

I was distracted from what Red was saying. A man's voice at the next table sounded familiar. I turned and looked at him, but did not recognize the face. He was about thirty, clean-shaven, and well-dressed. He and a friend had finished eating. As they left, the one man clapped a straight-brimmed hat on his head, and suddenly I knew who he was.

'Where you off to, Ben—'

I got up so fast that my chair turned over. I rushed out of the dining room and caught up with the man on the boardwalk outside. Seeing him in the half light there dispelled the last of my doubts that this was the man who had robbed me.

I tapped him on the shoulder. 'We have business down at the marshal's office, mister.'

'I beg your pardon, young man,' he said.

'You remember me, don't you?' I asked.

'I can assure you I have never laid eyes on you before,' he said.

'You laid more than your eyes on me four or five weeks ago,' I said.

97

The man's friend moved toward us. 'What's this about, Bob?'

I said, 'I'll tell you what, mister. You return my money and my watch, and I'll forget the whole thing.'

'You're mad,' the man said, 'absolutely mad.'

I grasped the lapel of his coat. 'We'll talk this over with Marshal Coe. Come on.'

His voice shook when he said, 'I'm going nowhere with you.' He tried to pull back, and we struggled. His friend grabbed me from behind.

The man behind me threw an arm around my throat and pulled. I let loose of the man named Bob. Bob tried to run, but I got my foot under him and he tripped and sprawled headlong into the street.

I wrenched the man's arm loose and turned and struck him. My fist snapped his head back, and his knees buckled. I lunged into the street after Bob. He was within my grasp when I heard an explosion and immediately thought someone had hit me from behind. A woman screamed. I felt confused and wondered why I was lying in the street.

'Ben! Ben!' Red knelt beside me. I wanted to sit up, but could not. Warm liquid ran down my back.

For a moment everything was too clear. I saw Red snatch away the derringer from the man who had shot me. I looked at the man who had robbed me, and I tried to point at him. He backed away. I tried desperately to speak, but no sound came from my mouth.

Red aimed the derringer at the man who had robbed me. 'Stay where you are, dandy.'

'I had nothing to do with this,' he said.

'Then you ain't got no reason to run off,' Red said.

Time slipped away from me. I heard Red say a doctor was on his way and I should not worry. Then I was aware of someone lifting my coat up and holding a lamp close to the wound in my back. Red told me the doctor was here. My own voice sounded far away when I asked: 'Am I dying?'

'Not today,' the doctor answered.

CHAPTER TWELVE

The doctor opened his black bag and brought out a bottle containing amber liquid. He opened it, poured some into a spoon, and made me drink it. The medicine tasted bitter, like bad whiskey, but in a few moments I became alert.

I raised up on my elbows. The knot of onlookers peered down at me. Several held lanterns. Presently Marshal Coe and a deputy came through the crowd, asking what had happened.

I pointed to the man named Bob. 'He robbed

me about five weeks ago, Marshal.'

'He's a mad man!' Bob shouted.

The man who shot me agreed. 'He's crazy, all right, Marshal Coe. I shot him in self-defense.'

'In the back?' Red asked.

'Hold on,' Marshal Coe said. He looked at the man who shot me. 'What's your name?'

'Carlson, George Carlson.' He pointed down at me. 'This fellow tried to kill me, and then he went after Bob. He's strong as a bull. If I hadn't shot him, he'd have killed both of us.'

'What's your last name, Bob?' Marshal Coe asked.

'Spicer,' he said. 'Me and George were standing here talking when this madman jumped us. I've never seen anything like it.'

Marshal Coe looked down at me. 'Seems like I remember you. Your name is Madison, ain't it? You was slugged and robbed a while back.'

'By that man,' I said. 'I recognized him.'

'As I remember, you never got a good look at the man who slugged you. It was too dark.'

'I know he's the man,' I said. 'I remember his voice. I remember that flat-brimmed hat, too.'

Marshal Coe shook his head. 'That ain't much proof, Madison.'

'He's out of his head,' Bob Spicer said. 'There's no telling who he'll jump next.'

Marshal Coe looked at me thoughtfully, then asked what had been stolen. I told him.

100

The marshal's eyes, along with the peering eyes of the onlookers, went to Bob Spicer. His hand shot to the watch chain on his vest.

'What kind of watch was it?' Marshal Coe asked.

I described the engraving on the cover and the wedding portrait inside the cover.

'Let's see that watch of yours, Mr Spicer,' Marshal Coe said. 'Maybe we can get this cleared up.'

Bob Spicer shook his head.

It was too much for Red. He lunged and jerked Bob Spicer's hand away, yanking the watch from his vest pocket. As soon as I saw it, I knew it was the gold watch Mother had given me. Red handed it to Marshal Coe. He looked at the engraving by the light of a lantern, then opened the cover.

'It appears you have this man's watch, Mr Spicer.'

'No!' he shouted. 'Those ... those are my folks in that picture!'

'Well, you come along with me and explain the situation,' Marshal Coe said. 'You, too, Carlson.'

'I don't understand this, Marshal,' George Carlson said. 'I just don't understand it.'

'In that case, I'll explain it to you in private,' Marshal Coe said. 'Come along.'

The doctor asked Red and another man to pick me up and carry me to his office. The wound burned as though a hot iron was pressed against my back. As I was lifted into the air, my eyes passed over the silent onlookers who gawked at me. Among them was Walter Hayes Taylor. The young woman beside him suddenly blurred in my vision, like a white apparition.

The rest of the night was lost to my memory. I woke in the morning on a cot in the doctor's office and learned that the bullet had been removed that night. The doctor had me moved to a small boardinghouse. He changed my bandage. As he did so, he told me that the heavy sheepskin coat I had been wearing had saved me from more serious injury; that, and the small caliber of the gun, he added.

Red visited me in the afternoon. He was still angry with me for running after Bob Spicer and taking two men on by myself. Red had guessed I had seen a friend and did not follow until he heard a shot.

'You probably saved my life, Red,' I said. 'There was another bullet in that derringer. I know I shouldn't have gone after Spicer alone, but all I could think about was getting my watch back.'

'It must be mighty important to you,' Red said.

'It is,' I said. 'That pocket watch belonged to my father. My mother died last summer. On her deathbed she asked me to return the watch to him.'

'So the man you're looking for is your

father,' Red said. 'And you think he's in Cloud City?'

'I heard that he was,' I said.

'Well, who is he?' Red asked. 'I can ask around and maybe track him down for you.'

'I doubt it,' I said. 'He's John Fox.'

'The only man I've heard of by that name is an outlaw,' Red said, grinning.

'That's him,' I said.

Red's grin faded. 'You're joshing.'

I shook my head. 'No one else knows about it, Red. I know I can trust you with the secret.'

'Sure you can,' Red said. 'Man, ain't this something. That outlaw is your old man. What does he look like? I've never seen a real picture of him.'

'I don't know how he looks now,' I said. 'The only photograph I have is that wedding portrait. It is nineteen years old.'

'That don't help much,' Red said. 'I was thinking he might be somewhere in camp, living under another name. You are.'

I smiled at the irony of it. Red asked the same question Judge Madison had asked me: What was I going to do to learn where John Fox was? I still did not know.

'Well, I'll keep my ears open,' Red said. 'If I hear anything, I'll let you know. Sometimes word gets around the Rocky Mountain Boys' Saloon.' He got up and said he'd better let me get some rest.

'Thanks, Red,' I said. 'Thanks for saving my

103

life.'

Red waved a hand at me. 'Aw, you'd have done the same for me.'

I slept hard and late into the next day. The boardinghouse was run by a widow named Mrs Hale. She took good care of me, looking in from time to time, and she brought bowls of broth.

In the evening I had two visitors: Red and Marshal Coe. The Marshal handed the gold pocket watch to me. He said he had gone through Bob Spicer's belongings, but had not found a money belt nor even much money. He had found a length of pipe wrapped in leather.

And Marshal Coe had learned that Bob Spicer was a poor gambler. He was deeply in debt. Spicer confessed to slugging several other men over the past few months. He often chose drunk miners and stole their pokes.

During his first night in jail, Bob Spicer had tried to hang himself with his own belt. A deputy had discovered him in time and saved his life.

Red asked, 'What about that George Carlson, Marshal?'

'That's up to you, Ben,' Marshal Coe said to me. 'The way I get the story, Carlson and Spicer were not partners in slugging men and robbing them. They're both clerks in stores here in camp. They've been friends for a few weeks. George Carlson apparently didn't know what Spicer was up to. Spicer backs up

104

the story. Carlson wishes he'd never gotten mixed up in it.'

'He's a low-down back-shooter,' Red said. 'He damn near killed Ben.'

'If you sign a complaint, Madison,' Marshal Coe said, 'I'll bring charges against Carlson. There are plenty of witnesses who saw him shoot you while you were going after Spicer. If the case goes to court, George Carlson will likely be on his way to prison.'

'I won't sign a complaint,' I said.

'Ben!' Red exclaimed.

I said, 'I think Carlson got in over his head. He thought he was helping an innocent man.'

Marshal Coe nodded. 'That's how I see it, too.'

Red was disgusted. 'Ben, you're giving that back-shooter more than he deserves.'

'George Carlson has a lawyer,' Marshal Coe said. 'I'll tell him to stop by here tomorrow. You can work out a financial arrangement to pay your doctor bills and so on.'

After the marshal left, Red told me again I was letting Carlson off too easy. I reminded Red that I had already lost a lot of time in my search for my father. A trial would only mean more lost time.

Carlson's lawyer came the next day at noon. He was a fat, smiling man who asked about my health. I ignored his small talk and told him what my intentions were.

'While my client is not a wealthy man,' the

lawyer said, 'I can assure you that he is prepared to return your generosity. Mr Carlson will pay your medical bills related to this injury, as well as your living expenses during your recovery.'

'That's fine,' I said. 'Goodbye.'

The lawyer glanced at me irritably. 'I'll draw up a document so stating and bring it to you to sign.'

I nodded.

'I realize you must not feel kindly toward my client—'

'That's right, I don't,' I said.

'Yes,' the lawyer said slowly. 'Mr Carlson is grateful that you're not pressing charges. He was considering thanking you personally.'

'We have nothing to talk about,' I said.

The lawyer moved to the door. 'I understand. I'll relay the message to my client.'

The following day Marshal Coe came back with the lawyer. After I signed the paper, the lawyer left.

Marshal Coe said, 'I talked to several witnesses who saw you take on Carlson and Spicer. They said when you hit Carlson, you about took his head off. He's still got a knot the size of an apple where you tagged him.'

'All I wanted to do was get him off me while I went after Bob Spicer,' I said.

'You did that,' Marshal Coe said. He paused, then said, 'I could use a man like you, Ben. Would you be interested in wearing a badge in this camp?'

I shook my head. 'I'm a hunter, Marshal. Bringing in meat is a safer way of making a living than bringing in prisoners.'

Marshal Coe grinned. 'I'll grant you that. Well, if you ever change your mind, stop by my office.'

'Thanks for the offer,' I said.

By the third day I was restless and began trying to move around the room. When the doctor came, he told me my restlessness was a good sign. I was healing. But he warned me that I could do nothing more strenuous than walk around the room for at least two weeks. Injured muscles needed time to heal, and the wound needed time to close. I would have to control myself or risk doing permanent damage to my back.

I told the doctor I would try, but at that time two weeks seemed like forever. To make matters worse, the doctor assured me I would have to stay off a horse for two months.

Red came by to tell me he was leaving in the morning. He said he hoped to see me when he returned in about two weeks. I tried to repay Red the money he had spent on the two mules he bought for me, but he would not accept it. I argued, but he would not change his mind. We shook hands and I thanked Red again for all he had done for me, but he shrugged it off and would not admit he had done anything out of the ordinary.

Though I was well cared for and comfortable, I came to hate the room in the boardinghouse. I memorized every wrinkle and pattern in the wallpaper, an unlikely design of flowers and vines, and I studied every dead fly on the windowsill.

Mrs Hale brought me copies of the Cloud City *Chronicle*, and I began searching them for mention of John Fox. Among the stories of fights and shootings in camp, the coming railroad, a man frozen to death in his small tent, the suicide of a prostitute by taking laudanum, and silver production figures from the mines, were several accounts of road agents. I read these word by word, but found no reference to the Fox gang.

The *Chronicle* reported the many cases of claim jumping in the mining districts and lot jumping in camp. Fights erupted over parcels of land and often resulted in killings. In the camp itself thievery was common. Anything that was not nailed down might be stolen. One resident wrote to the *Chronicle* to say that at last he had found a way to stop the firewood thieves. He drilled holes in selected pieces of firewood, filled them with blasting powder, then carefully plugged the holes. The man who stole a chunk of this wood, the resident wrote, would soon meet his maker.

The *Chronicle* also noted the comings and goings of the many celebrities and statesmen who visited Cloud City. Some came for investment purposes; others came simply to see the richest silver camp in the world.

A United States senator from New England visited the Taylor Mine. At one point in the tour, the senator saw a miner chewing a large piece of jerked venison. The senator asked him what he was eating. With no trace of a smile, the miner said it was the arm of an infant, and offered to share it. Another miner commented that food was scarce in Cloud City.

By the end of two weeks I had become a difficult patient. I was restless and short-tempered. Mrs Hale came to my room only to bring meals and the evening newspaper. I often thought of the irony of being imprisoned here while the man who shot me was free. And it was I who set him free.

At last Bob Spicer found freedom, too. A small article in the *Chronicle* reported that he had somehow come into possession of a shard of glass. He had cut both wrists and bled to death in the night.

I had had no visitors since Red left, so when there was a soft knock on my door, I expected to see Mrs Hale come in. The door opened slowly.

'Hello, Ben,' Casey said.

CHAPTER THIRTEEN

I was too surprised to speak for a moment. What finally came out of my mouth was little more than a mumble, like the first time I saw Casey. She was not the same girl now. Casey was a woman, and she dressed like a wealthy one. Her long coat was of soft white fur, and her skin-tight leather gloves seemed to have been made for her slender hands.

'Does the doctor allow you to have visitors?'

'I allow them,' I said. 'Come in. Bring that chair over here and sit down.'

Casey pulled off her gloves a finger at a time, removed her coat, and brought the straight-back chair close to the bed. She sat down gracefully, holding her coat on her lap.

'Every time I've seen you in Cloud City you've been in trouble,' Casey said lightly. 'I didn't know you were a troublemaker.'

'Sometimes I go a whole day without making trouble,' I said.

'Is your wound healing?' she asked.

'The doctor says it is,' I said. I added, 'You know, I think I saw you that night. Were you in the crowd?'

Casey nodded. 'I was afraid you were dying.'

'The thought crossed my mind, too,' I said.

'Why did that man shoot you?' Casey asked.

I explained briefly what had led up to the

110

incident.

'Then that day that you were thrown out of the Cloud City Hotel,' Casey said, 'you were looking for the man who robbed you.'

'That's right,' I said.

'Oh, Ben,' Casey said, 'I knew you needed help. I wish—'

I suddenly became annoyed with her sympathy and regrets. I interrupted her: 'I saw your father once, Casey. He looked well.'

'He has his good days and his bad days,' Casey said. 'He told me he had invited you to have supper with us at your convenience. You never showed up.'

'I work as a hunter,' I said. 'I don't spend any more time in camp than I have to.'

'I thought there might be another reason,' Casey said. 'I thought you might be avoiding me. Were you?'

'Why do you think that?' I asked.

Our eyes met and held for a long moment. 'Your question answers mine.' Casey looked away and added, 'I made a bad impression on you when we first met.'

'Forget it,' I said.

Casey brought her left hand to her carefully groomed hair in a motion that was probably not a conscious one, but it was one that effectively displayed a large diamond on her ring finger.

'You're married now,' I said.

'Not exactly,' Casey said, quickly covering

her left hand with her right. 'I mean, not yet. I will be soon.'

'Congratulations,' I said.

'I'm marrying Mr Taylor,' she said.

'Walter Hayes Taylor?' I asked.

'Yes,' Casey said. 'Have you heard of him?'

'I believe everyone has, Casey,' I said.

'He's well known in the East, too,' Casey said.

'Good for him,' I said.

A look of anger flashed across her face. 'You're being sarcastic, Ben. Mr Taylor is a fine man. He's been very good to my father and me. He got an office for Father. And he saw that we got a suite in the Cloud City Hotel.'

I said nothing to Casey. She took a deep breath and went on, 'Actually, it is partly because of Mr Taylor that I'm here. I remember that your true name is Benjamin Fox and you came to Colorado to look for an outlaw named John Fox. I imagine he's your father or your uncle. He's probably your father.'

Reluctantly, I nodded.

'I'll keep your secret,' Casey said, 'if you'll keep mine.'

'About your engagement?' I asked.

Casey nodded. 'Mr Taylor is still married. He plans to announce the divorce this month. Afterward, we'll be married, and then we're going on a long honeymoon to Washington, D.C. and Paris, France.'

'Is that what you came here to tell me?' I asked.

'Oh, no, I'm sorry, Ben,' Casey said. 'I must sound terribly boastful. I'm just so excited.'

'That's understandable,' I said.

'Oh, Ben,' Casey said. She reached out and put her hand on my arm. 'Everything I say seems to come out wrong.'

'What was it that you wanted to tell me?' I asked.

Casey leaned back in the chair. 'Mr Taylor rarely speaks of business matters in the presence of ladies, but during dinner a few days ago, the name of John Fox came up. Mr Reston was with us. Apparently Mr Reston and John Fox are bitter enemies. Do you know who Mr Reston is?'

'I've heard the name,' I said.

'He built the new smelter in Stump Town,' Casey said. 'I think he owns a few mines in the Stray Horse district. Anyway, John Fox came here to destroy him. He sent Mr Reston a note that said the Fox gang would stop the first trainload of smelted silver that left Stump Town. Did you know that?'

'No,' I said.

'Then you don't know where your father is,' Casey said.

'No,' I said. 'Do you?'

'Of course not,' Casey said. 'Mr Reston would like to know. He wants that outlaw captured.'

'Killed, you mean,' I said.

'What?' Casey asked.

'Reston's reward posters say dead or alive,' I said.

'Mr Reston is a very kind man,' Casey said. 'He would never order a man killed, if that's what you're saying.'

'I'm glad to hear that,' I said.

'Now you're being sarcastic again,' Casey said. She stood. 'Ben, you've changed. You really have.'

My own anger came to the surface. 'So have you, Casey. You look like you own the place.'

Casey blinked. 'I only came here to visit you and try to cheer you up, Ben.'

'I wonder,' I said.

'Wonder what?'

'You said Reston wants to know where John Fox is,' I said. 'Too bad you didn't find out from me.'

'Do you think I—' Casey stopped. 'Oh, Ben, how could you believe that I came here to betray you?' Casey folded her fur coat under her arm and whirled away. She left the room, the heels of her lace-up shoes hammering against the floor like rapid gunshots.

I was angry and glad she was gone. But I found no satisfaction in my anger. My temperament as a patient grew worse as the days wore on. At the end of the third week I pronounced myself mended and left the boardinghouse over the protests of the doctor.

He tried to exact a promise from me that I would stay off my horse for another month, but I only promised to stay out of horse races for a few days.

I wandered around camp for the better part of a week. Before Casey's visit, I was beginning to doubt that John Fox was anywhere near Cloud City. But if Alexander Reston believed he was here, that was good enough for me.

I spent some time in every gambling house and saloon in camp, thinking that if John Fox were here, men would be talking about him. But I heard nothing, and by the time I ran into Red at the Rocky Mountain Boys' Saloon, I was ready to return to my cabin. I asked Red if he wanted to see the place. He did.

We bought enough supplies to hold us several days, including fishing line and hooks, and rode out of Cloud City on the road that led up Stray Horse Gulch. The ride over Snowshoe Mountain was a painful one. I had told Red I was healed up, but when he saw me sweating and grimacing, he realized I was not.

'You should have stayed in camp, Ben,' he said.

'Another hour down there and I'd go crazy,' I said.

Red grinned at me and said dryly, 'I believe you misjudged the time.'

'I'll be all right,' I said.

'You don't look all right,' Red said.

When we reached the cabin at

115

midafternoon, Red forgot about me and became interested in the cabin. He walked all the way around, then went inside.

'Whoever built it did a right smart job of work,' Red said. He looked up. 'I can't say much for the roof, though.'

'That's my work,' I said. 'I'd never put a roof on a house before.'

'I can see that,' Red said.

'If you think you can do a better job,' I said, 'you're welcome to try.'

'I thought you'd never ask,' Red said. 'Start the cookfire, Ben. I'm getting hungry. Don't you lift nothing heavier than a skillet, hear?'

Red picked up my ax and walked into the trees. Presently I heard him chopping wood. He felled a pine tree, cut the branches off, and dragged it to the cabin. He cut it for length. The log was about six inches thick. I watched him climb to the roof and clear off the small trees and branches I had placed there. When he came down and started to lift the log to the top of the cabin, I moved to help him, but he growled and waved me away. Single-handedly, he lifted the log up and set it on top of the cabin.

While I built up a fire and fixed supper, Red elevated the ridge pole and secured it with rafters he fashioned from smaller trees. He began covering the roof with boughs, but did not finish. The smell of ham and eggs and fried potatoes and boiling coffee brought him down.

116

While he ate, Red looked up at the roof and complained mildly that the pitch needed to be steeper to shed the winter's snows.

'I don't plan to spend the winter here,' I said.

Around a mouthful of ham and eggs he said, 'This here wouldn't be a bad place to winter—if you liked being alone plenty. You could pack in one of them little iron stoves and about six foot of stovepipe, and you'd be set.' He repeated, 'It would be lonely, though.'

'I'm beginning to think I'm better off that way,' I said.

'Why's that?' Red asked. Part of an egg yolk ran into his beard as he spoke. Red dragged a hand across his chin, found the yolk, and vigorously rubbed it in.

'I don't know,' I said. 'Nothing goes right when I'm with people.'

'Everything goes right with you and me,' Red said.

I said, 'Everybody gets along with you, Red.'

'The hell,' he said. He stuffed his mouth with steaming food and added, 'You worry too much, Ben.'

'I guess I do,' I said.

Red washed down his food with several long gulps of hot coffee. Then he fired his pipe and leaned back against a wooden box that we had carried supplies in.

'A man told me once that free advice was worth what it cost—nothing,' Red said. He laughed. 'I've got some free advice for you,

117

Ben. You want to hear it?'

I nodded.

'You came out here looking for your father, didn't you? What are you going to do after you find him?'

'I don't know,' I said.

'My advice is that you ought to be thinking about that,' Red said.

'All I can think about is finding John Fox,' I said.

'I know it,' Red said. 'And it's got you wound up tighter than an eight-day clock, Ben. A man needs more than one thing to think on. You see what I'm getting at?'

'Yes,' I said.

'Good,' he said. 'You think on it. Now, what are you going to do to find your father?'

'Marshal Coe offered me a deputy's badge,' I said. 'I've been thinking about taking him up on it. I might hear something in camp that would lead me to John Fox.'

'Maybe,' Red said doubtfully. 'I've got an idea that you might not have thought of.'

'What?' I asked.

'Do you know what the Stump is?'

'It's a little saloon in Stump Town,' I said. 'I remember riding past it on my way to Cloud City.'

'There's talk that it's a hangout for road agents,' Red said. 'Did you know that?'

'No,' I said. 'Is it true?'

'I think so,' Red said. 'Plenty of those road

118

agents work on that stretch of road at the bottom of the pass. Stump Town would be a likely place for them to go.'

'I'll look into it,' I said.

'I thought you'd want to,' Red said. 'But be careful, hear? You go asking too many questions around there, and somebody might get nervous and plug you on general principles.'

I said I would be careful, but I knew one thing: If I did not start asking some questions, I would never get any answers.

CHAPTER FOURTEEN

Red and I stayed at the cabin for three days. Red finished the roof, then took my door apart and rebuilt it and fashioned a latch for it. We caught several trout in the stream that ran through the valley. When we had enough for a meal, we'd return to the cabin and coat the trout in corn meal and cook them. They curled in the frying pan and tasted better than any fish I'd ever eaten. On the morning of the fourth day we woke and found an inch of snow on the ground.

Red and I parted, wishing one another good luck. Red was vague about his plans. Though he had said nothing, I knew the railroad was on his mind and I wondered if he intended to leave

Cloud City for good. He rode in the direction of Snowshoe Mountain. I went up a ridge in the opposite direction and dropped into a gulch that would eventually lead me to Stump Town. Hunting in these mountains had taught me a great deal. I knew the landmarks to look for to keep my bearings, and I knew the shortest way to Stump Town from the cabin.

The sky cleared later in the morning, and the sun soon melted this first light snow. Birds sang and darted from one tree to another as though greeting spring. I followed the unnamed gulch until I was in sight of Stump Town.

A dark, foul cloud hung over the town. I rode into it and went straight to the Stump, a log cabin with a canvas roof. A black stovepipe chimney stuck out of the center of the canvas. Inside, the saloon was dark and rank, with the smell of cigar and pipe smoke and the sweet-sour smell of spilled whiskey.

I moved slowly until my eyes adjusted to the half light; then I stepped around the pot-bellied stove and went to the plank bar. The only light in the place was a lamp at the end of the bar. A Negro bartender was there, talking to a small group of men. They looked at me, measured me, then resumed their talk. The bartender moved a pace toward me and asked what I wanted. I ordered a mug of beer.

I heard low voices behind me. I looked through the gloom and saw two tables of men playing cards. These men did not look like

120

those at the bar. The men who clustered at the end of the bar were smelter workers or men who worked at the charcoal ovens. The men playing cards were all armed, and several wore flashy clothes.

The bartender charged me fifteen cents for a nickel mug of beer, then went back to his friends. I was within earshot of them, and soon learned that none of them were working now, but hoped for steady work in one of the smelters. One speculated he might go to Cloud City; another replied that a man might just as well be broke in Stump Town as in Cloud City.

I spent a long day in the Stump and ate supper there. I sat at a table near the pot-bellied stove and ate a bowl of the hottest chili that had ever battered my mouth. The bartender had ladled the stuff out of a large iron pot and had brought it to me with a chunk of hard bread that had mold on one end. The first bite of chili brought tears to my eyes and fire to my throat. The fire seeped through my stomach and smoldered there. I tried to put it out with three mugs of beer, and failed.

In the evening the Stump filled with workers from the smelter. They drank thirstily, fought drunkenly, and were gone by midnight. The last of the men who played cards left then, too.

I had boarded Sun King in a livery stable near the Stump and had bribed the owner into letting me sleep in his loft. As long as I did not smoke and was willing to pay two dollars a

121

night, he was glad to have me. I crawled into the loft shortly after midnight. I did not wake until long after sunup.

I spent the next afternoon in the Stump. The Negro bartender grew curious about me and began making conversation. He spoke of the weather and the coming railroad. If the railroad got no farther than Stump Town, his saloon would enjoy a boom. But come spring when the crews went to work again, the boom would subside. The railroad giveth and the railroad taketh away, he concluded.

'Most men around here are looking for work,' he said. 'When they don't find it, they usually move on to Cloud City.'

'I've been there,' I said.

'Oh,' the bartender said, as though I had answered a question. 'Likely you'll be heading over the mountains before long.'

'Not yet,' I said. Leaning closer to him, I said, 'I'm looking for a man.'

'You a lawman?' he asked softly.

'I didn't say I was hunting a man,' I said. 'I'm looking.'

'Who?'

'John Fox,' I said.

The bartender laughed. 'Ain't you something.'

'Have you seen him?' I asked.

'He don't come in here,' the bartender said.

'How do you know?' I asked.

'You're talking to the wrong man,' he said.

'I don't think so,' I said.

'Listen,' he said, 'you must be new to these parts. John Fox is what you might call a hero to the workers around here. These men who work in the mills and smelters all day are making rich folks richer. When a rich man gets robbed by John Fox, these men feel good about it. If they knew a man was after Fox, they wouldn't take it kindly.'

'I'm not after him,' I said. 'I have something that belongs to him. After I return it to him, I'll leave.'

'What thing?' he asked.

'That's between John Fox and me,' I said.

The bartender shook his head. 'I can't help you.'

But something in his manner made me suspect he could help me. Maybe he did not know John Fox, but he might know someone who did. Anyway, I thought, if he repeated what I had said to enough men, the word might finally filter down to the Fox gang. All I could do was wait and see.

The next day at noon I took on another bowl of chili. The saloon was nearly empty until three men came in and took a table in the far corner. These men usually played poker there, but now they drank from shot glasses and watched me. I had finished eating and ordered another mug of beer when one of the men left the table and came to mine.

He wore a flashy shirt and shiny trousers.

Strapped low on his right hip was a revolver in a cutaway holster. He pulled a chair out, turned it backward, and sat across from me.

'Who are you?' he asked.

'I'm Ben Madison. Who are you?'

He did not answer, but said, 'What do you want with John Fox?'

'I'll take that up with him,' I said.

The man clenched his right hand into a fist and tapped the tabletop hard enough to jiggle the empty chili bowl. When he turned his head slightly, I saw that half of one ear was gone and a long white scar ran around the back of his neck.

'I'm making this my business, Madison.'

I said, 'All you need to know is that I have something that belongs to John Fox. I came here to return it to him.'

'What is it?'

I gave him the same answer I had given the bartender yesterday: 'That's between us.'

The man grinned. 'Well, cut me in, Madison.'

'You're short on manners,' I said. 'If you know John Fox, tell him I'm here. Otherwise we have nothing to talk about.'

I was nervous and tried not to show it. The palms of my hands sweated, and I dragged them across my trouser legs.

'You've got a lot of mouth, Madison,' the man said. His right hand slowly drew back across the table, like a snake.

'Before you reach for your gun, mister,' I said, 'you ought to know that mine's pointed at your middle.'

The man looked down at the tabletop as though trying to see through it. He failed. His right hand stopped and flipped over, palm up.

'I never had such an idea,' he said. 'You're right about one thing. We ain't got nothing to talk over.'

The man stood. He turned and went back to his friends. I watched him snatch his hat off the table, heard him mumble a single command to his friends, then all of them left.

The Negro bartender said, 'That was some bluff. I could see your hand was plumb empty.'

My hands were shaking. I got up and carried the chili bowl and beer mug to the plank bar.

'You've got sand,' the bartender said. 'Costain's a killer. What would you have done if he'd called your bluff?'

'I'd have asked you to shoot him,' I said.

He shook his head. 'Ain't you something.'

'Does Costain know John Fox?' I asked.

'Some folks say he does,' the bartender said. 'I wouldn't know.'

'Sure,' I said. 'It doesn't pay to know things like that.'

'You've got it right,' the bartender said.

The following afternoon Costain came into the Stump alone. He moved across the dirt floor and stopped at the bar several feet away from me. I tried to read his face to find out if he had come to fight or talk, but couldn't.

'Get your horse, Madison. We're riding.'

'To where?' I asked.

'You can do this the easy way or the hard way, Madison,' he said. 'One way or the other, you're coming.'

I sensed that he had been given a job to do and did not like the assignment. I nodded and drank the last of the warm beer in the mug I had been nursing for the past hour.

As I followed Costain out the door of the Stump, someone jammed a gun barrel into the small of my back. Costain grinned and took my revolver from me. I looked at Sun King and saw that my rifle was gone from the scabbard. The man who held me at gunpoint was a scraggly-bearded man I had seen with Costain yesterday.

'Madison,' Costain said, 'you ride between me and Ike. Don't do nothing funny. I got orders to bring you in alive, but that won't keep me from winging you if you try something. And you can bet I'll put a bullet in the one place you don't want one.'

'Where are you taking me?' I asked.

'Mount up,' Costain said.

We left Stump Town, following the road that led toward the mountain pass. In little over a mile out of town I saw how much progress the railroad had made. The crew was here, laying a bed for the rails. At the rate they were going, they would be in Stump Town in a

126

few weeks if the weather held.

Ike led the way. Costain stayed behind me. Presently Ike turned his horse and rode upslope into the forest of lodgepole pines. I followed until Ike stopped in a small clearing. Costain reined up beside me. He pulled a bandanna handkerchief from his pocket and blindfolded me with it. Then he tied my hands to the saddle horn with a short length of rope.

I lost track of time and distance. As we rode through the thick forest, I was slapped by pine branches. My face stinging, I leaned forward in the saddle. We broke into open country and I felt the warmth of the sun on my shoulders and back. I straightened up in the saddle, but soon we entered the forest again. I was struck by a branch that might have slapped me out of the saddle if my hands had not been bound. Costain laughed.

Later I heard Costain speak. A voice far off to one side answered. At first I thought we had reached our destination, but as we rode farther on, I realized we had passed a sentry.

We stopped. I heard voices and smelled smoke from a fire. Costain yanked the blindfold from my face, knocking my hat to the ground. He untied my hands.

'Climb down,' Costain said.

I swung my leg over and dropped from the saddle. We were deep in the forest. At least half a dozen military tents were scattered through the trees. Cookfires blazed near several of

127

them. I saw a few men moving about, laughing and talking to each other.

Costain led Sun King to a line where several horses were tied. I bent over and picked up my hat. As I did so, I heard the flap of the nearest tent open. When I straightened up, I saw that a man had appeared.

He was slender and handsome. I watched him glance about, nod at Costain, and then his eyes met mine. His hair was cropped short, making him appear much the same now as he had in his wedding portrait nineteen years ago.

John Fox closed the distance between us, his tall, polished boots crunching softly on the dried pine needles that covered the ground. As he drew close, I was nearly overcome by the emotion of the moment.

I brought the gold pocket watch from my trouser pocket and held it out to him. 'I am Benjamin Fox. Before Mother died, she asked me to give this to you.'

John Fox's expression changed little as he opened the cover of the watch and looked at the photograph. After a moment he looked at me.

'I thought you had the name of Madison.'

'I took that name when I came to Colorado,' I said. 'No one out here knows who I am.'

'Then I reckon you don't, either,' John Fox said.

'I'm your son,' I said.

John Fox shook his head slowly. 'I always

128

wondered what they were going to tell you when you got old enough to ask questions. They didn't tell you anything, did they?'

'What are you talking about?' I demanded.

John Fox stared into my eyes. 'Your natural father is Horatio Madison.'

CHAPTER FIFTEEN

'I don't believe you,' I said.

'I thought you knew,' John Fox said. 'Costain told me your name was Madison.' He looked me over and added, 'You're even built like the judge. Is he still alive?'

I nodded in reply, but I was still numbed by what he'd told me. I mumbled that I didn't believe him because Mother had never said anything to me.

'Judge Madison probably told her the truth would ruin her social standing,' John Fox said.

I nearly struck him. But when I raised my fist, he only smiled.

'Is that why you came here?' John Fox asked.

At that moment I did not know why I had come. My thoughts were jumbled, and I had the odd sensation of standing apart from myself. For an instant I thought I was viewing this scene from a distance. Sudden laughter from a group of men in the forest brought me back to earth.

John Fox said, 'That estate where you grew up, Benjamin, was built by my father. I came back from the war in '65 and found my wife with a baby who couldn't have been mine. I left her. I left all my property, too. Do you understand?'

'I don't understand anything,' I said.

John Fox gestured to the tent he had been in. 'Come inside. I reckon we both could use a drink.'

I saw him look past me and say, 'It's all right.' I turned and saw Costain. He leaned against a pine tree a dozen feet away, his revolver aimed at my back.

I said to John Fox, 'You thought I came here to kill you?'

He only shrugged in reply. 'Come on,' he said.

In the tent were two military cots. I sat on one while John Fox poured brandy into two tin cups. He handed one to me and sat across from me on the other cot.

'I don't know what stories about me you've heard over the years,' John Fox said, 'but now you can hear the truth if you want it. Do you?'

'Yes,' I said.

John Fox was stunned and enraged at what he found when he came home from the war. He forced Mother to tell him who the baby's father was, then he left the estate and rode straight to Judge Madison's house. Under

130

threat of death, the judge admitted that he had taken advantage of the young woman whom he had known since childhood. Judge Madison offered to pay five thousand dollars if John Fox would accept the infant as his own.

'I declined his generous offer,' John Fox said dryly. 'I had good reason to kill him on the spot. I'd seen captured documents that proved Madison had directed the Yankees to secret food caches in Richmond. I figured he had been well paid for his treachery. I decided to either get some money out of him, or kill him. That was when he told me of the payroll at the bank.'

Judge Madison was an officer of the Atlantic Bank & Trust, and he knew that a Yankee payroll was being held there. The payroll was not heavily guarded because the Yankees were planning to move it the following day and did not want to draw attention to the money. The judge gave John Fox the key to the back door of the bank as well as the combination to the vault. That was how John Fox was able to get the drop on the guards, open the vault, and get away with the payroll in a matter of minutes.

'Madison thought he had bought me off,' John Fox said. 'He figured I'd take the money and go out West. But I went home that night. I gave the money to your mother and showed her where to hide it in the fireplace. At the time I figured I might come back someday. I didn't want her to sell off the property.'

131

I realized the currency Mother had given me must have been the last of that Yankee payroll. We had lived on it all those years—that, and the money from the sale of the tobacco land.

I told John Fox of Mother's death. 'She died asking for your forgiveness.'

'I should have gone back,' John Fox said. 'Everything might have been different.' He paused. 'I was young and proud. I had been wronged in the worst way imaginable. God, I was enraged!'

'You didn't kill Judge Madison,' I said.

'He alerted the Yankees,' John Fox said. 'I believe it was his plan to have me shot down in the bank. But no one thought to look for me at home. I had learned in the war that you can stay alive by doing the unexpected.'

John Fox refilled our cups with brandy. He asked who had come to the funeral, about Mattie and Abraham, and about the property that had once been his. I told him the best land had been sold off a few acres at a time, and that now Judge Madison was executor of the estate.

'He'll turn another dollar there,' John Fox said.

We soon ran out of things to talk about. We sat in silence for a long while. I almost told him of the time I had ridden with Stallcross and had seen ten men murdered from ambush. But I thought better of it and kept silent. I finished the brandy and told him I would go now.

John Fox nodded. I ducked out of the tent.

He came out behind me and followed as I walked to the line where Sun King was tied. My rifle was in the scabbard and my gun belt was across the saddle.

John Fox watched me strap on the belt, then asked, 'Who do you believe, Benjamin—Judge Madison or me?'

I told him the truth: 'I don't know.'

John Fox nodded. He asked, 'Are you going back to Richmond?'

'Yes,' I said.

'I wish I could go with you,' John Fox said. 'Sometimes I feel like I've been homesick for eighteen years.'

The remark surprised me. 'You didn't have to become an outlaw.'

John Fox shrugged. 'Once you start, you can't quit.'

'Why?' I asked.

He smiled. 'If you find the answer to that one, Benjamin, come and tell me.'

I stepped up into the saddle. Costain walked through the trees, leading his horse. He mounted and rode close to me.

'Benjamin, you'll have to be blindfolded again,' John Fox said. 'I'm sorry. If it was up to me alone, I wouldn't do it. But the lives of a dozen men are at stake.'

I looked back at the tents scattered through the trees. 'What are you planning to do?'

John Fox exchanged glances with Costain. 'I aim to make a man named Reston sorry he ever

133

tried to kill me.'

Costain leaned over and tied his bandanna tightly around my eyes. He pulled the reins from my hands. Costain did not bind my hands to the saddle horn this time. I felt Sun King move beneath me.

When we stopped, Costain pulled the bandanna from my eyes. I saw that we had reached the road that led to Stump Town and Cloud City.

'Ride out,' Costain said. 'Don't look back.'

I did not have to look back. I recognized this as being near the place where I had first met Red. The time now was early evening. I judged the outlaw camp was little more than an hour's ride from here.

I rode back to Stump Town, then followed the gulch into the mountains and returned to my cabin. Red and I had left some supplies behind. I found everything as I had left them, and for a time I had the pleasant feeling of returning home.

In the cabin that night I lay awake, staring into the darkness. I thought back over my boyhood and tried to recall an event or remark I had heard from Mother or Judge Madison that would give me a clue to the truth. Though I had not said so to John Fox, his account of what happened back in 1865 made more sense to me than anything I had heard from Judge Madison.

I thought I could understand how Judge

Madison had convinced Mother to keep the secret of my birth from me. He must have told her that he would help raise me and educate me. He would be a father to me in fact if not in name. The infant need never know the truth. The truth, Judge Madison might have said, would only poison my spirit and turn me against them.

I recalled that last evening in Judge Madison's study. I told him I could not rest until I found my father. In reply Judge Madison had murmured, 'Is that all that's bothering you?' Perhaps he was close to telling me the truth then. But he didn't.

And then early the next morning Judge Madison had driven his buggy to the Fox estate. At the time I had thought he had come to renew his argument. Now I wondered if he had decided to tell me the truth at last.

In the cold darkness of the cabin that night I remembered Mattie saying I would find things out. I saw her remark in a different light now. She must have known John Fox had been away from the estate too long during the war to have been my natural father.

I slept fitfully until dawn. I woke with a new thought in mind. Mother had been in her right senses when she gave me the currency and the gold watch. She had said the watch must be returned to John Fox. Was she sending me away from Judge Madison and from my home to discover the truth? For now I realized that my search was more than a search for my father. I was searching for the truth and for myself. I had found the truth.

I kept busy with routine chores that day. I laid in a supply of firewood. I added another layer of pine boughs to the roof. As Red had said, all the cabin needed now to be livable was a stove and a bunk.

By the afternoon of the second day my supplies were low. I saddled Sun King and rode to Cloud City under a gathering storm. Dark clouds boiled overhead like threats. By the time I reached Stray Horse Gulch, snowflakes floated through the air.

As I rode down Carbonate Street, I discovered I was thinking of Casey. I tried to close my mind off to her. I tied Sun King in front of the Reliable Hardware Store. I went in and priced some small iron stoves and stovepipe. I left without buying one. I walked to the general store and bought enough food to last a few days.

I walked out of the store and nearly ran into Marshal Coe. Stallcross was with him.

CHAPTER SIXTEEN

I almost made it. I got away from Marshal Coe with a nod and a quick exchange of greetings. Stallcross stared at me. I could tell he thought he knew me from somewhere but could not place me. I had untied Sun King and started to mount when Coe hailed me.

'Madison!'

For a moment I considered swinging up into the saddle and riding away. I wanted nothing to do with Stallcross. But as I watched the two men walk toward me, I decided to stay and face them.

'Do you know this man?' Coe asked, gesturing to Stallcross.

I nodded.

'He knows me, all right,' Stallcross said. 'I got a feeling he's tied up with Fox, Marshal.'

'Is there any truth to that?' Coe asked.

Suddenly I felt the need to stand up to Stallcross and defy him. I said, 'I was born with the name of Fox.'

Stallcross smiled. 'So that's it. John Fox is kin to you. And you gave me a phony name so I'd lead you to him, didn't you?'

When I did not answer, Marshal Coe asked, 'Are you mixed up with John Fox?'

'No,' I said.

'He's lying,' Stallcross said.

I turned away and put my foot in the stirrup and mounted.

'Hold it,' Stallcross said. 'You're not going anywhere until you tell me where John Fox is hiding.'

'I don't know,' I said.

Stallcross shook his head in disbelief. 'You

137

wouldn't have stayed in these parts this long if you hadn't found him.'

'Marshal Coe knows why I stayed here,' I said. 'You can talk to him about it, Stallcross.'

I mounted Sun King and rode away. Stallcross called after me, but I didn't look back. I made up my mind not to stop unless Marshal Coe spoke up. He didn't.

A light snow covered the ground. Snowflakes fell steadily from a murky sky. I turned up the collar of my sheepskin and buttoned the top button, thinking the winter's first big storm was here. I saw I was wrong when I topped Snowshoe Mountain. Far off in the distance the sky was clear. This storm would pass in a matter of hours.

Just as I went over the last ridge on the way to the cabin, I glanced back. I immediately wished I had looked sooner. A rider was trailing me.

Tracking me was easy for the rider. I knew it would be futile to attempt to lose him. I had to try something else. I urged Sun King ahead and rode down into the valley, straight ahead to the cabin.

I jumped out of the saddle, quickly stripped Sun King, and let him wander to the stream. I snatched my rifle from the scabbard and ran around the cabin into the trees. Keeping to the cover of the forest, I ran hard toward the ridge.

Cold air blasted into my lungs when I stopped in the pine forest. I tried to listen for the man's horse, but all I could hear was my own rapid breathing. Whoever had followed me would top the ridge and see the cabin. He would probably stop. Then he would either turn back or he would ride into these trees and sneak in for a closer look.

I caught my breath and soon heard the man coming. Seconds later I saw him. He rode slowly through the trees, peering intently ahead. He wore a serape around his shoulders and a sombrero on his head. A bandanna was tied over his ears against the cold.

The man drew close. As he passed by I ran through the trees toward him. I was a dozen paces away when I fired the rifle in the air and yelled.

As I had hoped, the horse reared. His rider grabbed for the horn. I took the rifle by the barrel and swung. The stock caught the rider flat across the back. He plunged out of the saddle and rolled. When he jumped to his feet, I recognized him.

'Alvarez,' I said.

Alvarez dug frantically around his serape. I lunged, trying to use the rifle to parry away his hand. But I lost my footing in the snow and went down, losing my grip on the rifle. At once I felt a sharp pain in my back and thought I had been shot again. Then I realized it was the old wound.

I looked up at Alvarez. He had drawn a knife. He looked at me and grinned.

139

'You have the knife, *señor*. Use it.'

I got to my feet and drew out my Bowie knife. My hip was light on one side, and I realized I had lost my revolver when I had fallen. Alvarez slowly moved toward me.

I had never been skillful with the Bowie knife. It had become my hunting knife, and the only thing I was certain of now was that it was sharp. Alvarez feinted and then made a swipe at me with his long-bladed knife. He missed and smiled.

As Alvarez moved toward me, I moved back. I backed into the branches of a tree and had to duck aside when Alvarez leaped toward me again. His foot slipped and for a moment he nearly fell. I took advantage of his imbalance and made a quick thrust. The point of the Bowie knife barely went through his serape and shirt, but it drew blood.

Alvarez went wild. He screamed and ran at me, slashing with the knife. The sheepskin coat probably saved my life again, because I felt the blade hit, but it did not cut.

Alvarez gave away too much weight. I threw him off me, and he flattened against a pine tree. He was dazed long enough to give me time to draw back my fist and hit him on the jaw. Alvarez slid to the ground. I kicked his knife away from him.

I walked back to the spot where the fight had begun and found my revolver in the snow. I holstered it and picked up my rifle. When I got back to Alvarez, he was slowly rubbing his face.

'Do we have to kill one another?' I asked.

Alvarez shook his head. Holding a hand to his chest where I had cut him, Alvarez got to his feet. I asked a question that I thought I knew the answer to.

'Why did you follow me?'

'Stallcross told me,' Alvarez said. He looked around at the dark green pine trees with their speckled covering of snow. 'It is cold here. Too damned cold.'

I said, 'Things are going to get hot if Stallcross doesn't leave me alone.'

'He says you know where the Fox is,' Alvarez said.

'You go back and tell him he's wrong,' I said.

Alvarez looked around again. 'I will go home, I think. I do not like this cold.'

I didn't know whether to believe him or not. I said, 'Tell Stallcross what I said.'

Alvarez nodded.

I watched him pick up his sombrero and catch his horse. He climbed into the saddle, took a look back at me, and then rode through the forest the way he had come.

The snow fell lightly until dark. The clouds broke up, and I saw stars overhead. Sun King came out of the trees and stood near the cabin. I went inside and turned in early.

Before going to sleep, I thought back over

141

the day's events and tried to understand their consequences. I suspected Stallcross would hound me as long as I stayed near Cloud City. My instinct was to warn John Fox that Stallcross was here. But if I did, I would be playing into Stallcross's hands. John Fox probably needed no help from me. The best thing I could do would be to leave Cloud City.

The future was dark and uncertain. I thought I might go back to Richmond, but at once I realized I had no desire to. My life there was behind me now. If I returned home and confronted Judge Madison with his past sins, what would be accomplished?

While I knew nothing would be gained by going back to Richmond, I did not know what else I could do. I fell asleep, wondering what was in my future.

I was wakened at first light by the cold touch of a gun barrel on my cheek. I opened my eyes and saw that the revolver was held by Wade Gibson. He knelt beside me. Stallcross stood by him, looking down at me.

'You're causing me trouble,' Stallcross said. 'You damned Foxes are always causing me trouble.'

I tried to move away from the barrel of the revolver. Wade Gibson growled at me.

I said, 'I'm trying to stay clear of you, Stallcross. You and your kind.'

Now Stallcross knelt beside me and leaned close. 'You cut Alvarez. I don't know what else

142

you did, but you didn't gain nothing by running him off.'

'I didn't run him off,' I said. 'He didn't like the weather up here.'

Wade Gibson jammed the revolver against my cheek and prodded me with it. 'You've got a smart mouth on you.'

Stallcross said, 'When is John Fox going to meet you here?'

'He isn't,' I said.

Wade Gibson moved the barrel of his revolver to the side of my nose. 'You ever seen a man with his nose shot off? Makes him look funny.'

I said, 'Call your dog off, Stallcross.'

'You might answer my question,' Stallcross said.

'I did,' I said.

'That wasn't a very good answer,' Stallcross said.

'It's the best I can do this early in the morning,' I said.

Wade Gibson cocked the revolver. 'Goodbye, nose.'

A long, tense moment passed before Stallcross said, 'All right, that's enough, Wade. Get up, Fox. Pull your boots on.'

I got out of the blankets and dressed. When I buttoned my coat, Stallcross motioned for me to go outside. He followed, closing the door behind him. Wade Gibson stayed inside.

Stallcross took me around the cabin and into

143

the forest. Two horses were tied there. Stallcross untied one and climbed into the saddle. He told me to mount the other and ride through the forest toward the ridge.

'Where are we going?' I asked.

'No talking,' Stallcross said.

I understood his intentions. Stallcross believed John Fox would come here sooner or later. He left Wade Gibson behind to ambush him.

The morning sky was pale gray. Yesterday's storm had left two inches of snow on the ground. By the time we rode down Stray Horse Gulch, Cloud City was coming awake. The morning air was fragrant with wood smoke from many stoves and cookfires.

We crossed Carbonate Street and rode to the back of the Taylor House and tied the horses there. Stallcross pointed to a door marked 'Private' and told me to go in.

The door opened to a long carpeted corridor. At Stallcross's direction, I walked the length of the hallway and knocked on the last door.

'Come in.'

I entered a richly furnished office. A crystal chandelier was suspended over a large desk that was cluttered with papers. In the leather-covered chair behind the desk sat a small man with a big mustache.

Stallcross said, 'This is Benjamin Fox, Mr Reston.'

144

'Any trouble?' Reston asked.

'No, sir,' Stallcross said.

Reston nodded. 'Get a bite to eat, and go back up there.'

'Yes, sir,' Stallcross said. He backed into the corridor and pulled the door shut.

'Sit down, young man,' Reston said in a friendly way.

'I'll stand,' I said. 'I won't stay long.'

'You're free to leave any time,' Reston said. 'But I wish you'd stay and hear us out.'

'Who?' I asked.

'Some friends of mine,' Reston said. 'Please stay. I have breakfast coming. You must be hungry.'

Reston was going out of his way to be friendly. I wondered why. He kept his right hand out of sight behind the desk. I wondered if he held a gun there and would stop me if I tried to leave.

I decided not to challenge him yet. I sat in a chair beside the desk. 'Stallcross and Gibson are wasting their time. John Fox isn't coming to the cabin.'

Reston smiled. 'So you have talked to your father.'

'No, sir,' I said. I made a lame effort to turn his verbal trap against him. 'If you'd tell me where he is, I'd like to speak to him.'

Reston laughed. 'You can relax, Benjamin. I didn't bring you here to make you confess anything. All I ask is that you hear me out.'

I heard a tap on the door. The door opened and I saw a waitress roll a cart in. The office was immediately filled with the tantalizing smells of cooked food and hot coffee. The waitress handed one tray to me, the other to Reston. She poured coffee, set the silver pot on the desk, and rolled the cart out of the office.

I wanted to resist the food, but couldn't. The breakfast was scrambled eggs, sausage, hot muffins, and jam. I wolfed all the food down and drank three cups of coffee. In an amused way Reston said he wished he could eat like that.

In half an hour they arrived, eight men richly dressed in dark suits, well groomed, and wearing jeweled rings on their fingers. The last man to enter was Walter Hayes Taylor.

'Gentlemen,' Reston said as he pointed to me, 'I present to you the son of John Fox.'

All of the men looked at me as though I were a newly discovered animal species. One man asked how I had been caught.

'I have a man in my employ by the name of Stallcross,' Reston said. 'He has my highest recommendation in case any of you should want to use him.'

Walter Hayes Taylor had been standing in the back of the office. Now he moved close to me. 'Where is your father, young man?'

Reston said, 'Let me handle this, Walter. You see, Benjamin claims to have no knowledge of his father's whereabouts.

Marshal Coe advises me that Benjamin may be telling the truth.'

'Then what's he doing here?' one bearded man asked.

Another said, 'Does this Stallcross believe him?'

'Stallcross is convinced Benjamin knows where his father is,' Reston said.

Walter Hayes Taylor said, 'Where the hell does that leave us?'

'Gentlemen, gentlemen,' Reston said, raising his hand. 'Hear me out. Stallcross recently captured a member of the Fox gang. He caught this man at the Stump. For those of you who don't know, the Stump is a low saloon in Stump Town. Known road agents have been seen there. The man Stallcross captured was shot to death when he tried to escape.'

'That wasn't smart,' a man said.

'It couldn't be helped,' Reston said. 'The man was leading Stallcross to the gang's hideout. He tried to get away and had to be stopped. However, this man had given some information to Stallcross. John Fox, gentlemen, plans to steal the first load of silver bullion that leaves here on the new railroad.'

The men were stunned. Then they all tried to speak at once until Reston quieted them.

Walter Hayes Taylor said, 'We must locate that gang and rout them! How strong are they?'

'I don't know,' Reston said. 'I would guess about twenty men.'

'Guessing won't do us any good,' a man said. 'We'll need an army to protect that train.'

Others said that was impossible. One man suggested that John Fox would very likely send his own men to be hired for the job. The discussion became confused and aimless. Reston looked on, amused. At last he spoke.

'I have a plan that may be workable, gentlemen,' Reston said.

'Let's hear it!' Walter Hayes Taylor said. He impressed me as a man who spoke needlessly, as one who had a firm grip on the obvious. He seemed to be only tolerated by the others, particularly Reston.

'You shall, Walter, you shall,' Reston said. He placed his elbows on his desk and leaned forward. 'My plan is twofold. First, I want to start a secret fund. The money will be used to hire a few good gunmen to combat these outlaws if it comes down to that. The gunmen will be recruited by Marshal Coe and Stallcross. Their good judgment should eliminate the danger of being infiltrated by Fox's men.'

Reston paused. 'Second, I plan to have the governor offer amnesty to John Fox and absolve him of the crimes he has committed in the state of Colorado.'

This brought cries of outrage from the men in the room. Still, Reston answered none of the questions flung at him, and he waited until their shouts of indignation had died down.

'I would remind you gentlemen that none of you has been hit as hard by the Fox gang as I have,' Reston said calmly. 'And I would remind you that John Fox is the one damned outlaw in this country who could almost put the Colorado & Western Narrow Gauge out of business. You know what that means to Cloud City. Civilization is coming, gentlemen. If we can't control the outlaw element, Cloud City's future is doubtful, to say the least.'

Walter Hayes Taylor said, 'I say, hunt the bastards down and hang them.'

'That's what I've said for the last several years, Walter,' Reston said. 'What makes you think you'll have more success than I've had?'

'Well, I didn't mean—'

Reston interrupted him. 'Gentlemen, the only sure way to stop the Fox gang is to retire John Fox. Remove him, and the gang will fall apart for want of leadership.'

'Will the governor grant amnesty to this outlaw?' one man asked.

Reston glanced at Walter Hayes Taylor. 'He will if Walter and I suggest it. Right, Walter?'

Walter Hayes Taylor smiled. 'He'd better.'

Another man said, 'What makes you think Fox would be interested in such a deal?'

'Now, you have touched the key question,' Reston said. 'We must get the answer to it, and soon.'

'How?' Walter Hayes Taylor asked.

Reston looked at me. 'I expect this young

149

man to act as courier between John Fox and me.'

CHAPTER SEVENTEEN

'I told you I don't know where he is,' I said.

Reston smiled tolerantly as his glance moved from me to the other men in the office. 'Gentlemen, I am doubling the reward for John Fox. At ten thousand dollars, there will be a greater temptation for a traitor in the outlaw gang to betray Fox's whereabouts.'

Walter Hayes Taylor drew himself up and shouted, 'Double it again! I'll add ten thousand myself!'

Several other men joined in, sounding much like bidders in an auction. Reston recorded each figure in a ledger. At last he totaled them.

'That's close enough to fifty thousand dollars,' he said. 'I'll kick in enough to make it fifty even.'

Walter Hayes Taylor said, 'At that price there ought to be men standing in line to backshoot Fox.'

'Now, Walter,' Reston said, 'it is not our purpose to order the killing of a man.'

This last remark was greeted with strained silence. I sensed that every man there agreed with Taylor, but did not wish to contradict Reston.

I knew Taylor was right. A fifty-thousand-dollar reward was a death sentence. I realized I had no choice now.

I said, 'I'll try to locate John Fox. But if you men don't hold off on that reward, I doubt if I can find him before a murderer does.'

A bearded man spoke up: 'Wouldn't that be too bad!'

Reston raised his hand in a gesture that asked for silence. 'Benjamin makes a good point. I suggest we allow him one week to relay our offer of amnesty to Fox. If Benjamin fails, or if Fox rejects the offer, we will post the reward. Agreed?'

The wealthy men of Cloud City reluctantly agreed to this plan, though I had no doubt they thought it was a needless concession to an outlaw.

Walter Hayes Taylor said, 'One week and no more, young man!'

Reston stood and came around his desk. He took me by the arm and guided me out of the office. 'Stallcross will be busy helping Marshal Coe hire men to bear arms against the outlaws. I assure you he won't try to follow you. I would regard it as a personal favor if you would send Stallcross back to me when you return to your cabin.'

Before I left, Reston wished me luck, as though we had entered into a business deal that offered mutual benefits. Perhaps he actually saw it that way. I did not.

I rode Wade Gibson's horse back to the cabin. The morning sun was bright in the clear sky, but did little to warm the air at this altitude. The horse's nostrils puffed twin clouds of steam with every breath.

I urged the horse over Snowshoe Mountain and then rode across the open valley to the cabin. Stallcross and Gibson came out of the trees.

'What did Reston tell you?' Stallcross asked.

'He wants to see you right away,' I said. 'You two won't be trailing me any more.'

Stallcross looked at me doubtfully. Having just come from Reston gave me a momentary advantage, and Stallcross knew it. He did not like it. Without another word he turned and walked back into the trees. Presently he returned, leading his horse. Stallcross and Wade Gibson mounted and rode off across the field of snow, retracing the tracks I had made. My anger boiled over as I watched them, and I felt a sudden and powerful urge to kill them both. I kicked the powdery snow and sent a sparkling cloud of it after them.

Stallcross and Gibson were only hirelings. Powerful men like Reston and Taylor used their great wealth to buy what they wanted. They bought men and used them. When Reston found a man he could not buy, he still was able to devise a way to control him. Reston had found a sure way to control me, one that cost a mere fifty thousand dollars.

I kicked another cloud of snow into the bright sunlight, disgusted with myself for delivering the message to Stallcross. I had run an errand for Reston.

I caught Sun King and saddled him and rode to Stump Town. I entered the Stump at noon. Sitting near the warm pot-bellied stove, I ate a fiery bowl of chili and drank a mug of beer. When the Negro bartender came to the table, I asked where Costain was.

The bartender looked at me as though I had asked whether the sun had risen that morning. 'I reckon you know better than me.'

'How do you figure that?' I asked.

'By adding up two and two,' he said. 'You rode off with Costain and lived to tell about it.'

The bartender must have told Stallcross that I had left the Stump with Costain. I asked the bartender if he knew Stallcross.

'Sure,' he said. 'I seen him and that other fella give Ike a beating. They done it right here. Then they tooken him outside and shot him through the head. Claimed Ike tried to run off. I reckon I would have, too.'

'Was Costain here?' I asked.

'Hell, no,' the bartender said. 'Costain, he would have chewed them detectives up and spit them out on the floor.' He added, 'None of them men with Costain have come in here since Ike got killed.'

When I left the Stump, I knew I would have to find the outlaw camp on my own. I thought I could, but I would have to take a roundabout way. I had no reason to accept Reston's word that he would not have someone follow me.

I left Stump Town, riding in the opposite direction from the main road. I took a narrow switchbacked road up a hillside that overlooked Stump Town. This slope was covered with the stumps of pine trees as though a giant had swept through wielding a scythe. From the top of the hill I reined up and looked back. The shacks and tents below were toys. So were the smoking smelters. The newest building had huge letters painted on its roof: RESTON. I felt as though he were watching.

I was not being followed, though. On these stump-covered hills all about, there was no place for a man to hide. I saw wagon traffic on the roads, but no single riders.

I rode Sun King down the far side of the hill, away from the stench of Stump Town, and made a wide circle back to the main road. I came out in a forest several miles below Stump Town. I rode directly to the place where Costain had removed my blindfold and ordered me to leave without looking back.

I turned Sun King and rode into the trees. There were no fresh tracks in the snow, but I believed if I rode in a generally straight line from here, I would be close to the outlaw camp in an hour.

As I no longer had a pocket watch, I had to guess the time. I rode through the forest and

154

into a ravine that was choked with brush. The brush slapped my legs, and I knew I had been here before. I rode out of the ravine and deeper into the pine forest. A tingling sensation shot up my spine, for I believed this was near the place where Costain had spoken to a guard. I searched the dark forest ahead, hoping to see the guard before he saw me.

I saw no one. I dreaded but expected to hear the sound of a gun being cocked. I did not hear it. Tension brought sweat to my face that quickly chilled and ran shivers through me. At last I realized I had to have passed the place where the guard was, and the outlaw camp was ahead.

In the forest I found blackened circles where cookfires had been laid, rectangles bare of snow where tents had been staked, and packed snow where horses had milled. John Fox had moved his camp.

I circled, looking for tracks leading away. There were few signs that a dozen men had been here. They had left no tin cans, bottles, or cigarette papers. In a week a man could ride through without ever knowing men had camped here.

I found too many tracks in the snow. In pairs, all the men had ridden away from camp in various directions. They must have agreed on a meeting place. The pairs of men would probably ride far away, then double back in a day or two and meet up with John Fox. I

155

wondered which set of tracks were his.

I had a sense of futility as I chose a pair of horse tracks and followed them through the snow. At some point, I guessed, the men would try to leave no tracks at all. If I lost them, I would have to come back and pick up another pair of tracks. A great deal of time would be consumed. A week could easily slide by, leaving me in this forest of pine trees, following tracks to nowhere.

The pair of hoofprints I followed led over a hillside to a stream in the next valley. The water ran swiftly here and had not frozen. The tracks led into the stream, but did not come out. I turned back and returned to the abandoned camp.

Another pair of hoofprints led me deeper into the forest. I rode for two hours. At the base of a high mountain, I could see the tracks leading over a saddle between two peaks. I reined Sun King up and turned back.

My reasoning was that John Fox would establish another camp within two hours' ride of the railroad. He would want men and horses to be fresh when they hit the train. If I was right, the tracks that led up the mountainside could only be a diversion.

It was late afternoon by the time I returned to the camp and picked up another set of tracks. I was determined to follow these until dark. I did. To my great surprise, they led me in a roundabout course back to Cloud City.

CHAPTER EIGHTEEN

I ate supper in the Taylor House and then walked next door to the Rocky Mountain Boys' Saloon. The saloon was not as crowded as at other times I had been there, and I began to realize that the whole camp was quieter tonight. Cold weather had driven the brass band and the gambling house barkers indoors. And apparently this first taste of winter had driven many men out of camp.

I stood at the long polished bar that gleamed in the lamp light and absently looked at my own reflection in the mirror as I thought back over the day's events. Tomorrow I planned to return to the outlaw camp. Tracking men in this fresh snow was too good an opportunity to pass up.

In the big mirror behind the bar I saw the reflected images of men playing poker at several tables. As I watched, I realized that one looked familiar. His back was toward me. Then he turned his head and I saw he was missing half an ear.

Costain had not seen me. He was intent on his poker hand. He picked up two cards, then discarded two others. He lost the hand.

For the next hour I watched the pile of chips before Costain grow and then shrink. The pile had grown again when he shoved his chair back and scooped the chips into his hat. He left the table and went to the caged office in the rear of the saloon. I saw him cash in the chips and pocket a handful of currency and coins.

I faced the bar as Costain passed by. In the mirror I saw him button his heavy coat, yank his hat down on his forehead, and go out through the front door. I followed.

Three quarters of a frost-white moon shone overhead, casting white light upon the snow. Costain walked along the boardwalk, half a block ahead of me. When he turned the corner at a side street, I ran to close the distance between us.

I stopped when I came to the corner. I took a quick look around and saw Costain trudging up the narrow street. I walked after him, my boots crunching loudly in the snow.

Costain angled across the street as he approached a large house surrounded by an iron fence. A lamp with a red globe burned in the window. The iron gate squealed when Costain opened it.

'Costain,' I said.

I had surprised him. That would have been a fatal mistake if he had not been wearing his heavy coat. Costain whirled to face me and fought the lower button on his coat as he dug for his revolver.

I raised my hands. 'It's me. Don't shoot!'

Costain stopped when he recognized me. 'I thought I'd seen the last of you.'

158

'So did I,' I said.

'What the hell do you want?' Costain asked.

'I have to see John Fox,' I said. 'Where is he?'

'I dunno,' Costain said. He added, 'You and him got your business finished.'

'Something else came up,' I said. 'I have to talk to him.'

'About what?'

'It's about Reston,' I said.

Costain asked suspiciously, 'What about him?'

I did not answer. 'Where is John Fox? If you keep me away from him, he's not going to like it when he finds out.'

Costain cast an uneasy glance at the second story of the big house, then looked at the white ground at our feet.

'He's in there, isn't he?' I asked.

Costain said, 'He don't want to talk to you.'

'Tell him I want to see him,' I said. 'If he won't talk to me, I'll leave.'

Costain looked back at the house. The windows on the second story were black. 'He ain't going to like this. Not one bit.'

'If I don't talk to him,' I said, 'he's not going to like it, either.'

'Come on,' Costain said.

I followed him up the walk to the porch. Costain twisted a bell handle in the door. The door was opened by a thin woman who wore a red velvet dress. Costain called her 'Maude.' She let us into a darkened room, lighted only

159

by the red light from the lamp in the window.

Costain told me to sit in one of the upholstered love-seats, then he and Maude left the room. I heard them go up a creaking staircase. From another part of the house I heard a woman's shriek, followed by shrill laughter.

I had a long wait. A few men came and went. Maude met them at the door and led them through the room. Most went up the staircase. I recognized one man. He had been in Reston's office. He passed by me with no more than a glance in my direction.

Later I heard someone come down the staircase. John Fox entered the room. His shirt was untucked, and he wore no boots.

'Come in here, Benjamin.'

John Fox led me into the hallway where the stairs were. We crossed the hall and went into the kitchen. John Fox turned up the lamp on the dining room table, then looked at me.

'What is it?' he asked.

I reminded him of our earlier conversation in the outlaw camp. 'You told me if I found a way for you to quit your way of life, I should come and tell you.'

John Fox smiled. 'You've found an answer to the great riddle?'

'Not exactly,' I said. I told him of Reston's offer of amnesty.

John Fox shook his head. 'It's a bluff. Reston wants me killed. He's trying to draw me out.'

'I don't think so,' I said.

'Reston has been trying to kill me for a long time,' John Fox said. 'He's had a killer named Stallcross on my trail for more than two years. He killed ten of my men about a month ago. I reckon he believed I was with them.'

'Why weren't you?' I asked.

'I knew something was wrong when we pulled five hundred dollars out of a strongbox that was supposed to have a payroll in it. I tried to talk the others into coming up here. Some of them did. But most of those ten men had their families in the Roost. They wanted to go home. Stallcross ambushed them.'

'I know,' I said. 'I was there.'

John Fox stared at me. 'Maybe you'd better explain that, Benjamin.'

I told him how I had met Stallcross in Denver and had decided to ride with him. I described what had happened at the Gate.

John Fox asked, 'How did you find out I was headed this way?'

'A dying man said you were here,' I said. 'His name was Sam Baxter.'

John Fox nodded and repeated the name. 'Sam Baxter.'

I changed the subject. 'Reston and Taylor and several other men have put up another reward for you. They've raised fifty thousand dollars for you, dead or alive.'

'I didn't know I was worth that much,' John

161

Fox said. 'They want me mighty bad, don't they?'

'Yes,' I said. 'They're afraid you'll bring the railroad traffic to a stop.'

John Fox grinned. 'That's a challenge.'

'Will you accept the amnesty offer?' I asked.

John Fox shook his head. 'It's a trick, Benjamin.'

'No, it isn't,' I said. But I wondered if my belief was the truth or only wishful thinking.

'If it is on the up and up,' John Fox said, 'why didn't Reston give you a copy of an amnesty proclamation?'

'There hasn't been time,' I said.

'A telegram from Denver doesn't take much time,' John Fox said. 'And why would the governor offer amnesty to me?'

'Taylor and Reston say that if they ask for it, they'll get it,' I said.

'But they haven't,' John Fox said. He repeated, 'This is a trick to bring me out in the open.'

I realized nothing I could say would make him trust Reston. I said, 'If I get a copy of the amnesty agreement, will you look at it?'

The question made John Fox squirm. He reached into his trouser pocket and brought out papers and a sack of tobacco. His hands quivered slightly as he built a smoke. He lit it, drew in, and then exhaled a cloud of smoke that swirled over the lamp on the table.

'I'd take a look at it,' he said at last.

I left after we agreed to meet here the next night. I felt a growing sense of excitement. Though John Fox did not trust Reston, he was interested in the deal that was being offered. Now I wondered if Reston would hold up his end of it. In the morning I found out.

For the night I took a room in a two-dollar boardinghouse. After breakfast in the morning I went to Reston's office. He seemed mildly amused that in only one day I had found John Fox.

'So he wants to see a document,' Reston said. 'Consider it done. I'll get a telegram off this morning. In forty-eight hours I should have an official amnesty agreement in hand. What else did John Fox say?'

'Nothing,' I said. I added, 'He doesn't trust you.'

'I once promised I would see John Fox in his grave,' Reston said. 'You can tell him I have no plan to keep that promise. If he'll retire from his life of crime, that is good enough for me.'

The door opened. Walter Hayes Taylor came in. When he saw me, he stopped.

'Come in, Walter,' Reston said. 'I have good news.'

Walter Hayes Taylor scowled. 'Well, I don't.'

Reston ignored the remark. 'It appears John Fox is interested in an amnesty agreement. I'm sending a wire this morning to urge the governor to draw up an agreement and send it

163

here by courier. I want you to telegram the governor, too. Insist that he get right on this.' Reston paused. 'Do you hear me, Walter?'

'I hear,' he said dully. 'I'll do it after the funeral.'

'Whose?' Reston asked. 'I haven't heard of anyone's death.'

'It's that doctor,' Walter Hayes Taylor said. 'That old phrenologist. You met him once or twice.'

Reston smiled. 'Oh, yes. The one with the daughter.'

Walter Hayes Taylor nodded. 'Pneumonia got him. I have to be a damned pallbearer.'

'You never were much on funerals, were you, Walter?' Reston asked.

'I hate the idea of it,' Walter Hayes Taylor said. He shuddered. Suddenly he became aware of my presence. 'Where is your old man, boy?'

'Now, Walter,' Reston said. He stood and came around his desk and spoke to me. 'Benjamin, you come back here day after tomorrow. I'll have that agreement right here on my desk.'

I left Reston's office. I walked along a side street to a funeral parlor. I went in and asked the mortician about the funeral of Dr Collier Moore. The mortician did not know, but he sent me to another funeral parlor off Carbonate Street. There I learned that the services were set for ten o'clock and the burial

164

would be at eleven.

The Cloud City cemetery was high on a hillside overlooking Stray Horse Gulch and the sprawling mining camp below. I walked up the hill and joined half a dozen mourners for the burial. The pallbearers appeared to be hired men. From their ragged clothes I guessed they were men who needed money. Walter Hayes Taylor was not among them. He stood beside Casey.

Casey wore a black dress and a black scarf. The black scarf made her face look as white as the snow on the ground. She clung to the arm of Walter Hayes Taylor.

I looked at Casey as she watched the coffin being carried from the hearse to the new grave. At the whispered directions of the mortician, the men lowered the coffin into the hole. Walter Hayes Taylor kept his face averted from the scene. When the first clods of dirt struck the coffin, he winced. Casey cried and leaned against him. I left, believing she had never seen me.

CHAPTER NINETEEN

After dark, I returned to Maude's. She recognized me and was very friendly to me. She led me back to the kitchen and poured a cup of coffee for me. Maude went upstairs to tell 'him'

165

I was here.

John Fox came into the kitchen and sat across the table from me. He listened intently while I told him of Reston's promise to have an amnesty agreement signed by the governor within forty-eight hours.

'What are the conditions of this thing?' John Fox asked.

'Reston didn't mention any,' I said.

John Fox said grimly, 'There'll be some.'

I did not reply, but it occurred to me that he should accept a few conditions. John Fox was one of the best-known outlaws in the West. Very few outlaws had been granted amnesty.

John Fox said, 'On the day after tomorrow, Benjamin, you ride to Stump Town. I'll be on the road somewhere. If everything is all right, keep a handkerchief tied around your neck. If something's wrong, don't wear it. Be sure nobody's trailing you.'

'All right,' I said.

'If you see Costain, don't mention any of this to him,' John Fox said. 'He thinks you're feeding me information from Reston.'

'That's what I am doing,' I said.

'About the train, I mean,' John Fox said.

I walked back to the boardinghouse and tried to imagine all the consequences of what was happening. There was a great deal I did not know. I suspected Reston was not putting all of his cards on the table. John Fox probably wasn't, either. I was in the middle. If anyone

166

needed to know what cards were being played, it was I.

I stamped the snow off my feet and went into the boardinghouse. I opened the door to my room and saw a folded sheet of paper on the floor. Someone had slid it beneath the door. I touched a match to lamp wick and picked up the sheet of paper and opened it:

Ben, I must see you tonight. Please keep the lamp burning by your window.

Casey

I moved the lamp to the table by the window, then pulled off my boots and stretched out on the soft bed. I was brought out of a light sleep by a knock on the door. I got up and opened the door.

'Hello, Ben,' Casey said. 'I saw you leave here yesterday. I found out which room you were in and left that note for you.'

'Come in,' I said.

Casey unbuttoned her coat and pulled it off as she entered the room. I was surprised to see her wearing the same dark, heavy dress she had worn on the train when we had first met. Her jewelry was gone. So was the large diamond she had worn on her ring finger.

'I'm sorry about your father, Casey.'

She nodded. 'Thank you for coming this morning.' She had seen me after all.

'Your father was a kind man. I think he

167

believed in the goodness of people,' I said.

'Yes, he did,' Casey said. 'But he was impractical.'

'Good men often are,' I said.

Casey sat on the straight-back chair and folded her coat across her lap. 'We shouldn't have come to Cloud City. Father wasn't strong enough for the winter here.' She repeated, 'We shouldn't have come.'

I wondered if she somehow blamed herself for her father's death. I sensed she was keeping something bottled up inside her. 'What are you going to do now, Casey?'

She looked up at me. Her lips quivered, and her rush of words came with tears. 'I'm leaving, Ben. Tomorrow. I hate it here. It's so cold, always cold ... everything's wrong here.'

'Where are you going?'

'I don't know!'

I moved to her and put my hands on her trembling shoulders. Casey stood and clasped her arms around me. Her coat fell to the floor between us. I held her until her sobs became soft murmurings.

When Casey spoke at last, her mouth was close to my ear. Her voice was steady. 'Everything went wrong, Ben. Mr Taylor never planned to take me anywhere. He'll never leave his wife. All he'll ever do is complain about her. I was a fool not to see that all along. I was a fool to let him use me.'

She paused and breathed deeply against me.

'He pretended to be a friend to my father. He gave us money when we needed it. But then he refused to help at the funeral. Afterward we had a fight, an awful fight. Everything came out. He said he could buy a dozen women like me. The worst part was that I knew he was right. He had bought me. I'm so ashamed, Ben.'

Casey had cried herself out. Now she was talked out. She rested against me for a long time. When she let loose, she stooped to pick up her coat. I reached for it, but was too late. She straightened up and put the coat on.

'I'm sorry to have burdened you with my grief, Ben,' Casey said. 'There was no one else I could talk to.'

She moved to the door and opened it. Casey did not say goodbye, but she looked back at me in a way that meant farewell. She stepped out into the hallway. I went after her.

'Casey, don't go.'

'What?'

'I don't want you to leave, Casey,' I said.

She looked at me for a long moment, then said, 'Nothing's ever gone right for us, Ben.'

'I've often wondered why,' I said.

'It's my fault,' Casey said.

'Don't blame yourself,' I said. I moved close to her and took her hand. 'I love you, Casey.'

'Oh, Ben,' she said.

She had spoken my name that way many times before. Now I realized I did not know

169

what she meant. I blurted, 'Do you love me?'

Casey nodded. 'Yes, I love you, Ben. I've been unhappy ever since we parted in Denver.'

We kissed long and hard in the hallway of the boardinghouse. At last Casey pulled away.

'Ben, I don't want to stay in this camp another day. Do you understand? I don't care where we go, but we have to leave.'

'I can't leave, Casey. Not yet.'

Casey shook her head. 'I need to get away, Ben. I have to sort things out in my mind.'

'I have a place,' I said.

I described the cabin to her. Casey said it sounded like a faraway place that was not far away. She was right. In the morning I agreed to come by for her at the Taylor House.

I rented a saddle horse for Casey early the next morning. Casey waited for me in the lobby of the Taylor House. All of her belongings were packed into one bag. To explain, Casey told me she was starting over.

We rode out of Cloud City on the mining road that led up Stray Horse Gulch. The day grew warm, and the sun reflected brightly off the snow. Once when I looked back at Casey I saw she was riding with her eyes closed, her face tilted up to the sun. Her horse plodded along behind Sun King. Late in the morning we reached the cabin.

The only tracks in the snow around the cabin were those of coyotes. No man had been here since I had left. I stripped the horses and hobbled them. Casey tentatively entered the cabin, then came back out.

'How do you like it?' I asked.

'When you said it was primitive, you weren't joking,' she replied.

I realized she had never had to live under these conditions. 'Casey, do you want to go back?'

'No, I want to be here with you.'

The clear weather held through the night and the next day. A warm wind came through the high country, and patches of earth began to show in the white fields of snow. The golden grasses lay matted against the ground, glistening with moisture. Wisps of steam lifted from the creek. Casey announced that Indian summer had come. We welcomed the season with love.

I talked to Casey more intimately and truthfully than I had ever spoken to anyone before. I told her of my boyhood on the Fox estate, of my break with Judge Madison, and of what I had learned from John Fox. Then I told her what was happening now between Reston and John Fox.

'I'll have to leave you alone here for a while,' I said. Casey nodded. 'I'd rather be alone here than alone in Cloud City.'

At noon I returned to Cloud City and went straight to Reston's office. True to his word, he had two copies of an amnesty agreement on his desk. The two sheets of parchment were

171

impressed with the seal of the state of Colorado, signed by the governor and countersigned by the secretary of state:

By the authority of criminal pardons vested in this office, I, George C. Abbott, Governor of the State of Colorado in the presence of John T. Young, Secretary of State, do hereby grant amnesty to John Fox and do hereby absolve him of guilt and prosecution from noncapital crimes he has committed in the State of Colorado upon agreement to the following conditions:

One: John Fox, by his legally witnessed signature, agrees to cease his life of crime and live in a peaceful and honest manner for the remainder of his days in the State of Colorado;

Two: John Fox agrees to have no association or keep company with known criminals or persons of criminal nature;

Three: John Fox shall be protected from extradition by court officers of other States so long as he resides peacefully within the borders of the State of Colorado;

Four: All outstanding rewards and bounties offered for John Fox shall not be payable from this date forward;

Five: This proclamation grants amnesty
        only to John Fox.

Reston asked me, 'Will he sign it?'

'I don't know,' I said.

'He's a fool if he doesn't,' Reston said. He pointed to the bottom of the document. 'John Fox's signature has to be witnessed by a citizen who is in good standing in the eyes of the law. If he lets some outlaw sign, this document will be worthless. You tell him that.' He added, 'And you can't sign it because you're related to him.'

'I'll tell him,' I said.

I left Reston's office and ate a meal in a cafe across the street. Early in the afternoon I took Sun King for a leisurely ride on the road to Stump Town. When I was certain no one was following, I tied my handkerchief around my neck.

I had rounded a bend in the road when I heard a horse come out of the trees behind me. I looked back and saw John Fox.

'Follow me,' he said.

We left the road and went through a stand of leafless aspen trees, then entered a forest of pines. Out of sight of the road, John Fox stopped. I unbuttoned my shirt and brought out the two sheets of parchment. I handed one to him and watched him read and reread it.

John Fox handed the document back to me.

'Won't you sign it?' I asked.

John Fox looked away from me. He stared into the trees for several moments. I heard a

173

wagon pass by on the road. Then it was quiet again.

'I'll sign it,' John Fox said at last.

'I hoped you would,' I said. I told him what Reston had said about witnessing the signature. I wondered aloud who we could find to do it.

John Fox said, 'I want Reston to witness my signing of this thing.'

CHAPTER TWENTY

'Why Reston?' I asked.

'It's fitting,' John Fox said. 'I want his signature right below mine on that document.'

'I don't know if he'll meet with you,' I said. 'He doesn't trust you.'

'Well, we're even on that score,' John Fox said.

'Where do you want to meet him?' I asked. 'In Cloud City?'

'Hell, no,' John Fox said. He made a sweeping motion around us with his hand. 'We'll meet in the great outdoors. This is where I've lived for the past eighteen years.'

I told him I doubted Reston would agree to such a meeting.

'That's the way it has to be,' John Fox said.

'If Reston doesn't agree to meet with you,' I said, 'he'll announce that fifty-thousand-dollar

174

reward. He'll send men out to hunt you down.'

'So be it,' John Fox said. 'If he wants war, he'll have it.'

I wished I could change his mind. I said we could easily find someone else to sign the document, but John Fox replied with a shake of his head, ending the discussion.

Before we parted, I arranged to meet him at Maude's the next night. In the meantime I would give his message to Reston. But as I rode back to the freight road, I was not optimistic that Reston would agree to such a meeting.

I returned to the cabin that evening. I showed the amnesty document to Casey. She read it with great interest.

'He is smart to have Mr Reston witness his signature,' she said. 'No one will ever doubt the authenticity of the agreement.'

'I don't think that's his reason,' I said. 'He seems to think of it as some kind of truce in a war. He wants to meet Reston like Lee met Grant. John Fox is surrendering, but he is not defeated.'

On the afternoon of the next day I went to Reston's office. He was not there. I waited outside his door for nearly an hour. When he arrived, Stallcross was with him.

Reston greeted me enthusiastically. He unlocked his office door and told me to go in. He stayed behind a moment and spoke to Stallcross. Reston came in alone and closed the door.

175

'Well?'

'He'll sign the document,' I said.

'Good,' Reston said. 'When?'

'Any time,' I said. 'He asks that you witness his signature.'

Reston looked surprised, then amused. 'What the devil for?'

'He says it's fitting,' I said.

Reston smiled curiously. 'Where does he expect this signing to take place?'

'Somewhere out of camp,' I said.

Reston shook his head. 'No. The answer is no.'

'I'll be there,' I said.

'So you can witness a murder?' Reston asked.

'John Fox has never killed a man,' I said.

'That's a popular myth,' Reston said. 'Men have been killed during the commission of his robberies. Fox may not have pulled the trigger. But he is responsible for their deaths, isn't he?'

I was suddenly jerked back in time, and for an instant I felt as though I were engaged in a discussion with Judge Madison. I did not know how to disprove what was being said, yet I did not want to agree.

Reston, having won an easy victory, went on, 'I'll tell you what, Benjamin: If John Fox will come here to my office, unarmed, I'll witness his signature.'

I shook my head. 'He won't come here, Mr Reston.'

Reston turned up the palms of his hands. 'Then my signature will never be on that amnesty agreement.'

That night I went to Maude's. As I had predicted, John Fox said he would not go to Reston's office under any conditions. And John Fox again said no when I suggested that we find someone else to witness his signature.

I left, frustrated and annoyed with both men. They acted like children, one stubbornly refusing to agree with the other. At the cabin that night I told Casey what had happened. Now Reston would post the reward, and John Fox would be a marked man in a matter of hours.

Casey said sadly, 'All because of their argument over a signature.'

'That's right,' I said.

Casey looked thoughtful. 'Ben, why don't you bring them here?'

'What?' I asked.

'Think of this cabin as neutral ground,' Casey said. 'The two men will come here alone. We will be here to make certain it is not a trap for either man. Isn't it worth trying?' She added, 'There may not be another chance.'

Casey was right. But I said, 'I don't want you involved in this.'

'I already am, Ben,' Casey said. 'I'm here with you. And I'm not leaving.'

I laughed and reached out and grabbed her. 'You're a good woman, Casey.'

In our embrace Casey said, 'And you're a good man. Isn't it wonderful that we're together?'

'Yes,' I said, 'it is.'

The next day I returned to Reston's office and told him of this new plan. He recalled that Stallcross had described my cabin to him. Then he complained that he had not been on a horse in months. Abruptly, he agreed to meet John Fox there.

'Stallcross can show me the way,' he said.

'But you'll have to come to the cabin alone,' I said.

Reston nodded. 'After he points out the cabin to me, I'll send him back to Cloud City. What time will Fox be there?'

'If he agrees to this meeting, I'll tell him to be there early in the afternoon.'

Reston opened a drawer in his desk and brought out a sheet of engraved stationery and an envelope. He scribbled his name on the envelope, folded the stationery and slipped it inside, and handed it to me.

'Leave this with the desk clerk at the Taylor House,' Reston said. 'I have to inspect the smelter this afternoon and won't be back until late. If there are any changes in this meeting you've arranged, write them down.'

'All right,' I said. Before leaving, I asked, 'Mr Reston, why are you doing this?'

'Agreeing to meet an outlaw?' Reston asked. He paused. 'Let's just say I have a sense of history. And John Fox may be right: It's fitting to have both our signatures on the amnesty agreement.'

I took a roundabout route to Maude's, making certain I was not followed. Maude answered the door. She held her red velvet robe together at the throat. She let me in when I asked for John Fox. He was in the kitchen.

John Fox questioned me closely about the cabin's location. He regarded this compromise doubtfully, but since the idea came from me and not Reston, he was not suspicious of it. While John Fox did not agree to meet Reston at the cabin, he did agree to look at the place the next morning.

I left, telling him to be at the head of Stray Horse Gulch at sunup. On the way out of camp, I stopped by the Taylor House and left a message for Reston. I wrote on the sheet of stationery that John Fox had agreed to meet him in my cabin tomorrow at noon. I hoped I was telling the truth.

In the morning I waited at the head of Stray Horse Gulch long past sunup. I watched the trail that angled down to the mining district, and grew more and more anxious. Presently I heard a voice behind me.

'What are you waiting for?'

I turned and saw John Fox standing in the trees a dozen yards away. I wondered if he had been there since sunup.

I asked, 'Don't you trust me?'

179

John Fox led his horse out of the pines and mounted. 'Old habits, Benjamin, old habits.'

We rode over Snowshoe Mountain, then left the trail and cut over the top of the ridge that led to the cabin. As we dropped down toward the open valley, John Fox stopped. I reined up and watched him study the treeline around the small valley. I realized he was looking for places of ambush. At last he asked how I had found the cabin.

'I stumbled onto it when I was working as a hunter,' I said.

'Has Reston been here before?' John Fox asked.

'No,' I said.

'Then how will he find it?' John Fox asked.

I hesitated, then said, 'Stallcross has been here. He'll bring Reston.'

John Fox's eyes shot to mine. Fire was in them. 'Stallcross.'

'Reston will ride in alone,' I said. 'He'll be here at noon.'

John Fox stared at me. 'You've got everything figured out, don't you? You figured that if you got me up here, I'd go through with this thing.'

I said irritably, 'You want Reston to sign the agreement. I'm bringing him to you.'

John Fox nodded. 'He'll have plenty of time to bring his army and set up an ambush.'

'I don't believe he will,' I said. 'But if you think that's what he's up to, you'd better ride

180

out now.'

We stared at one another, and for a long moment I feared that he would ride away. But then a movement across the valley caught his eye. I followed his glance. Casey had stepped out of the cabin. She stirred the fire and moved the coffee pot into the coals.

John Fox looked at me in surprise. 'Who's she?'

'Her name is Casey,' I said.

John Fox grinned. 'Hell of a name for a woman.'

'Why don't you tell her that?' I said.

'Not on a bet,' John Fox said. He kicked his horse and rode at a gallop all the way across the valley to the cabin. I followed. Casey saw us coming and waved.

I introduced Casey to John Fox. He asked what kind of lies I had to tell to get her to come to this lonely cabin.

Casey laughed and answered, 'It was my idea. Ben wanted to take me on his world travels, but I talked him into coming here.'

John Fox shook his head in good-natured disbelief.

I said, 'It was Casey's idea to have Reston sign the amnesty agreement here.'

'I should have guessed that,' John Fox said. 'Leave it to a woman to figure things down to a gnat's knee.'

Casey asked, 'Don't you like the way a woman can figure things?'

181

'Why, sure, I do,' John Fox said, laughing. He looked at me. 'This is some woman you've got, Ben.'

'I know,' I said.

The three of us sat around the fire and drank coffee beneath the morning sun. I had never seen John Fox in such good humor.

Shortly before noon, John Fox caught his horse. He bridled the animal and tightened the cinch.

'I believe I'll go for a ride,' he said.

Casey and I watched in silence as he swung up into the saddle and rode across the grassy meadow. He disappeared into the pine forest. Casey spoke the thought that was on my mind.

'Will he come back?'

At noon I saw two riders at the head of the valley. Even from this distance I recognized Stallcross in his canvas coat and in the slumped way he had of sitting his saddle. Stallcross turned back. Reston came in alone.

Reston reined up in front of the cabin. 'Well, where is he?'

'He'll be here,' I said, trying to sound sure of myself.

'It's past noon,' Reston said. He looked at Casey, then back at me.

I said, 'Step down. Have a cup of coffee with us.'

Reston shook his head. I saw him take a second look at Casey. 'Don't I know you?'

Casey met his eyes. 'I'm Casey Moore. You

don't know me, Mr Reston.'

Reston smiled and climbed out of the saddle stiffly. 'Yes, I do, Miss Moore. Walter wondered where you'd gone.' Reston looked at both of us. 'So you two got hooked up. The world is full of surprises, isn't it?'

'Here's another one, Reston.' John Fox spoke as he walked around the cabin, leading his horse.

Reston whirled. The two men stared at one another. Neither spoke, and a tense moment passed as they regarded one another like opposing generals in an uneasy armistice.

The tension was broken when John Fox said, 'We'll do this inside.'

We went into the cabin. John Fox came in last. He pulled the door shut. Casey picked up the lantern. Its wavering, pale light cast deep shadows into the faces of Reston and John Fox.

I had a pencil ready, but John Fox surprised me by reaching into his coat pocket and bringing out a pen and a small bottle of ink. He had planned ahead, while letting me think he had misgivings about meeting Reston here.

John Fox turned the signing into a strange ceremony. I handed one copy of the amnesty proclamation to him. He signed it, then handed it back instead of passing it to Reston. He signed the second one and gave it back to me. I gave them to Reston. Reston looked helpless for a moment until John Fox handed

183

his pen to me. I gave it to Reston. In all this time no one spoke. The loudest sound in the cabin was the scratching of the pen on the two sheets of parchment.

After Reston signed his name beneath John Fox's, he handed the documents back to me.

Reston said, 'One is to be kept by John Fox. The other is to be sent back to the governor.'

'I'll do that,' I said. I handed one copy to John Fox. He had taken off his hat and coat. Now he drew his revolver and pointed it at Reston's chest. Casey cried out.

'Take off your hat and coat, Reston,' John Fox said.

'What the devil are you talking about?' Reston demanded.

'Do it, or I'll put a hole in you,' John Fox said.

'I never should have trusted you,' Reston said as he removed his coat and hat.

John Fox tossed his own coat and hat to Reston. 'Put them on. You're riding my horse out of here. Ride out of this little valley the way you came in.'

'What the devil are you up to, Fox?' Reston asked.

John Fox smiled. 'I aim to find out how good a shot Stallcross is.'

'Hell,' Reston said, 'I sent Stallcross back to Cloud City.'

'Then you won't mind riding my horse and wearing my clothes, will you?' John Fox asked.

Reston swore softly. He put on the coat and hat. Both were too big for him. He looked like a boy in man's clothes, a boy wearing a theatrical mustache.

'This is an outrage,' Reston said.

'You're getting a good horse out of the deal,' John Fox said. 'Now, ride out.'

Reston threw the door open and left the cabin. John Fox motioned for Casey and me to stay inside. We watched Reston through the doorway. In another time, the sight would have been humorous. Alexander Reston, one of the wealthiest men in Colorado, mounted John Fox's horse, shoved the outsized hat out of his eyes, pushed a sleeve of the coat back over his wrist, and rode away.

When Reston topped the far ridge and left our sight, I turned around and looked at John Fox.

'I'll be damned,' he said.

CHAPTER TWENTY-ONE

'You were wrong,' I said.

John Fox spoke in a voice that was at once casual and bitter: 'Maybe Reston was telling the truth. I figured he had Stallcross out there laying for me.'

'You meant to send Reston to his death,' I said.

185

John Fox glared at me. The high tension of the last several minutes was still with us. It threatened to explode now. I had seen a side of John Fox that I did not like, and I felt a compulsion to tell him so. But the moment passed, and I said nothing more. John Fox did not defend his act.

I watched John Fox place the amnesty agreement in his shirt. He went outside to Reston's horse. Casey and I followed. We watched him lengthen the stirrups and then swing up into the saddle. He rode close to us.

'Good luck to you two,' John Fox said. He held his hand out to me.

I reached up and shook his hand.

'Benjamin,' John Fox said, 'thanks for bringing that watch to me. You did a good thing. I'm sorry I had to be the one to tell you about Madison and your mother.'

'You told me the truth,' I said.

He nodded, then asked, 'Will the truth make you free, like it says in the Bible?'

'I hope so,' I said. But I believed John Fox was the one who longed for freedom.

John Fox said goodbye again and pulled the horse around and rode into the trees, using the forest for cover. I wondered if the time would ever come when he could ride in open country.

That same day I went to Cloud City and mailed the copy of the amnesty agreement to the governor. I bought some supplies from a list Casey had made. As I was leaving camp,

Red hailed me from the boardwalk in front of the Rocky Mountain Boys' Saloon. He tried to talk me into staying in camp for the evening. I told him I had a powerful reason for returning to the cabin, and if he would come up for a visit, he would meet the reason.

The warm weather held all week. The snow on open ground melted away and sent glistening rivulets of cold water downslope. Runoff flowed over the solid ice on the creek in the little valley.

Red showed up two days after I had seen him in camp. He was shy and reserved around Casey. When Casey tried to joke with him as she had with John Fox, Red grew embarrassed and flustered.

Red brought a newspaper that told of the amnesty agreement between the state of Colorado and John Fox. I told him about the signing. Red asked what John Fox would do now. I told him I did not know. When he asked what I planned to do, I said I didn't know that, either.

I glanced at Casey. 'We're taking one day at a time.'

'This here Injun summer will do that to you,' Red said. 'There's something about this season that makes a man want to lay around and hope it will last forever.' He laughed. 'Then the snow hits. Well, Ben, you can always get through a winter by hunting. That mining camp down there has a big appetite year-around for fresh

187

meat.'

Red left that day. I watched him ride away, realizing I would probably never see him again. I would not see John Fox again, either. A part of my life had come to an abrupt end. Another part was beginning, but I did not understand much of it. What was ahead? I had no idea of what to do with myself besides live with Casey. I gave long and deep thought to an ancient question: Why can't a man live on love alone?

The next day I returned to the livery stable with Casey's rented horse. I settled up with the owner and got my three mules out of hock. The transaction hit my wallet hard.

I began hunting game again in the mountains above Cloud City. I had no trouble selling the quarters of meat to the slaughterhouse, but now my heart was not in the hunting. I began to feel regret about killing deer and elk. Dark thoughts entered my mind and lingered there, thoughts of why a man must kill in order to live.

In Cloud City I picked up a copy of the *Chronicle*. Much of the front page was still devoted to the pardoning of John Fox. It was big news throughout the state. The governor was quoted at length as he reminded the citizenry that John Fox had never been accused of murder; the governor asserted that he would have no part in granting amnesty to a killer.

Other articles in the newspaper gave many accounts of the Fox gang's exploits. John Fox

188

was often depicted as a kind of Robin Hood of the West. But other less fanciful articles told of the many people who had placed their life savings in banks, only to have their money stolen by the Fox gang.

A later issue of the *Chronicle* was filled with news of the Colorado & Western Narrow Gauge. The rail line was now complete to the smelters in Stump Town. The fair weather allowed an outdoor ceremony to celebrate this event. Food and drink were served at no cost. A brass band played. And finally a red ribbon was cut by the owner of the rail line in the presence of the smelter owners. Alexander Reston was one of them.

The next morning the first train rolled out of Stump Town, loaded with passengers and carloads of smelted silver. Among the passengers on this historic train were Mr and Mrs Walter Hayes Taylor, who were 'coursing along their merry way toward the fair southern climes where they would spend the winter.' The silver-bearing cars were guarded by 'skilled gunmen numbering nearly two score under the able leadership of Detective Stallcross.'

At noon of this day the telegraph lines were cut, the railroad tracks below Stump Town were dynamited, and Walter Hayes Taylor's bank in Cloud City was robbed of more than one hundred thousand dollars in currency and coin.

I later learned that Marshal Coe prevented

the bank robbers from making a clear escape. In a brief and deadly shootout on Carbonate Street, two outlaws were killed by Coe, and a third was wounded and captured. Marshal Coe himself was shot through the leg. One of the dead outlaws was identified as Costain, a man known to be John Fox's lieutenant.

The telegraph lines were repaired within hours of the robbery. A special train was dispatched from Denver and arrived at the damaged track by noon of the following day. The train carried the owner of the Colorado & Western Narrow Gauge and Walter Hayes Taylor. With Taylor came Detective Stallcross and twenty of the gunmen who had provided security for the train. Taylor himself had hired them at top wages. And he placed a fifty-thousand-dollar reward for the capture of John Fox, dead or alive.

Some of these events I learned by reading the *Chronicle*. Other details I learned from Stallcross. With Wade Gibson and three other men, Stallcross came to the cabin.

'The pass is sealed off,' Stallcross said. 'The railroad cut through the canyon is guarded by my men, too. I've got twenty men in these mountains. Every one of them figures to be a rich man by knocking John Fox out of the saddle.'

'Why are you telling me?' I asked.

'So you can tell Fox next time you see him,' Stallcross said.

190

'I'd bet he's long gone by now,' I said.

Stallcross shook his head. 'We've got him boxed in. One of the boys even got a shot at him.'

'Give that man a medal,' I said.

'You listen here,' Stallcross said, pointing his blunt index finger at me, 'there won't be no more pussyfooting around with you. If I ever find out you're protecting Fox, you're dead.'

'Stallcross, get off that horse,' I said.

'Do you aim to fight me?' Stallcross said, sneering. 'I don't have time for you.' He pulled his horse around and kicked the animal. Wade Gibson and the others followed him up the valley. One man peeled off and rode into the trees.

I turned around and saw Casey watching from the doorway. She said, 'I'm scared, Ben. What's going to happen?'

'We're not going to wait around to find out,' I said. 'Get packed. We'll leave tonight.'

Casey started into the cabin, then turned back. 'Where are we going?'

'Pick a place,' I said.

Casey smiled. 'Do you mean it?'

'Yes,' I said. I took her arm and led her into the cabin.

'I want to go to California,' Casey said.

'Then that's where we're going,' I said. 'We'll leave after dark.'

'This is so exciting,' Casey said, laughing.

I took her in my arms. 'Casey, marry me.'

191

'I wondered if you were ever going to ask me,' she said.

'I'm asking,' I said. 'What's your answer?'

'Do you want it here, or in California?' Casey asked.

'You're teasing,' I said.

'Of course I am,' Casey said. 'This is the greatest moment of my life. I want to make it last as long as I can.'

'Then you will marry me?'

'Yes, Ben,' Casey said. 'I will marry you.'

We rested until nightfall, then ate a cold meal. Casey packed all of our supplies and utensils. I went outside and untied the mules and brought them to the cabin. Casey would have to ride one until we got over the mountains and found a place where we could buy a saddle horse.

A sliver of the moon shone in the starry sky. It would give us enough light to find our way, yet not enough, I hoped, to expose us to Stallcross's men.

We were ready to leave when I heard someone whisper to me from behind the cabin. I drew my revolver and walked around the cabin. John Fox was there.

I whispered, 'Stallcross has a man around here somewhere.'

John Fox spoke in a normal tone of voice: 'I know. I just now conked him on the head.'

'Stallcross came here today,' I said.

'I saw him,' John Fox said. 'He's got men all

over these hills. I haven't seen anything like it since the war. Stallcross must have caught somebody. His men know where the hideouts are. I've been shot at twice in two days.'

I asked the question that nearly everyone in the state was asking: 'Were you in on that robbery?'

'No,' he said. 'Not directly.'

In the darkness I could not see the expression on his face. 'What do you mean?'

'It was my plan all along to hit Taylor's bank in Cloud City,' he said. 'The train was a decoy. That bank was wide open, except for Coe. Costain should have taken care of him. He was careless once too often.'

'Costain only carried out your plan?' I asked. 'You weren't there?'

'That's right,' John Fox said. 'Costain was plenty mad when I told him I had accepted amnesty. We'd been together for a lot of years, and I guess he felt left out. He must have figured if he could pull this robbery, I'd get the blame. He was sure right about that.'

'Why did you stay here?' I asked.

'If I run now, I'll have to keep on running,' John Fox said. He added, 'I'm here to ask your help, Benjamin.'

'How can I help?' I asked.

'You can talk to Reston for me,' John Fox said. 'Tell him I'm sorry about that little trick I pulled on him. Tell him the truth about the holdup. Maybe he can make Taylor pull in that

193

reward.'

'I can try,' I said. I did not say so, but I had little hope of success.

'Thanks, Benjamin,' John Fox said. He put a folded piece of paper in my hand. He said it was a message to the governor, and he asked me to send it by telegraph from Cloud City.

John Fox said we could meet again on the trail that led over Snowshoe Mountain. He had found a hideout near the mountaintop that gave him a long view from all sides. I agreed to be there the next day. Then John Fox was gone.

I turned around and saw the dim shape of Casey as she stood beside the cabin. 'You heard?'

'Yes,' she murmured. 'Ben, I love you.'

We went into the cabin and read John Fox's message by the light of a lantern. The words were carefully printed in pencil on the back of the new circular that Taylor had put out, offering fifty thousand dollars' reward for John Fox, dead or alive:

Governor Abbott, I had no hand in that robbery of Taylor's bank in Cloud City. Costain pulled that one. I am writing this to tell you I am a man of my word and I will never break the terms of my amnesty. W. H. Taylor has set this big reward on me, but he has no legal right to do it. If I have to be arrested while the robbery is being investigated, I will turn myself over to you,

194

but not Taylor or Stallcross or any of his men. I am ready to live the life of a law-abiding citizen, but I cannot do it with this big reward hanging over me like a damned noose.

John Fox

That night Casey and I rode to Cloud City. We took a room in a boardinghouse. In the morning I telegraphed a copy of John Fox's message to the governor, explaining who I was and how I had come into possession of it. Then I went to Reston's office.

CHAPTER TWENTY-TWO

As I had expected, Reston expressed disbelief when I told him John Fox had not taken part in the robbery of Taylor's bank. Reston pointed out the one obvious fact: The robbery was as well planned and almost as well executed as John Fox's other crimes over the years.

I told Reston that the plan to rob Taylor's bank had been devised by John Fox, but had not been carried out by him. The robbery had been committed by Costain and other members of the Fox gang. John Fox no longer had control over them. I asked if John Fox was to be held responsible for every holdup committed by a member of the Fox gang from now on.

Reston smiled. 'You'll miss your calling if you don't become a lawyer one day, Benjamin.'

I went on to say that John Fox did not act like a man guilty of pulling off one of the largest bank robberies of recent times. He had stayed here, risking capture, to prove his innocence.

Reston said, 'If what you say is true, John Fox could have saved us all a lot of trouble by telling us such a plan was in existence. He must have known the gang would try to carry out his plan.'

'He should have warned Marshal Coe,' I said. 'But by doing that he would have been a turncoat. That is something John Fox would never do.'

'I suppose you're right,' Reston said. 'But why hasn't he turned himself in?'

I reached into my pocket and brought out the reward circular that John Fox had given me. I handed it to Reston. After he had read the penciled message on the back, I said that John Fox sent his apologies for forcing Reston to wear his hat and coat and ride his horse back to Cloud City that day.

Reston asked with half a smile, 'Would Fox apologize if he were not in need of my help now?'

'I doubt it,' I admitted. 'John Fox was convinced you'd try to have him killed.'

A strange expression crossed Reston's face. He looked down at the desktop and was silent for a long moment. 'I once made a threat that I'd see Fox in his grave. That was a mistake, and I regret it. I don't blame Fox for distrusting me.'

The admission showed him to be a better man than I had thought. And Reston was twice the man John Fox judged him to be.

I asked, 'Will you help him?'

'The damned truth is,' Reston said slowly, 'there isn't much I can do now.'

'You could ask Taylor to withdraw the reward,' I said.

Reston shook his head. 'Walter's madder than a cat set afire. He wants Fox.'

'But you and I know Taylor is using an illegal reward to order a murder.'

'In reality, Benjamin, it is now beside the point whether or not the reward is legal,' Reston said. 'It's done.'

'The governor can revoke it, can't he?' I asked.

From Reston's sympathetic expression, I realized my question was naïve. 'Governor Abbott owes a great deal to Walter.'

Reston stood. 'I'll speak to Walter about this reward. I doubt if he'll change his mind, but I'll do what I can.' Reston handed the circular back to me. 'My advice to John Fox is for him to do what he says he is willing to do. He should turn himself over to the governor before this amnesty proclamation is officially

197

reversed.'

'Will that happen?' I asked.

'A number of important men in this state are pressuring the governor to do just that,' Reston said. 'Many people believe John Fox is simply using this amnesty agreement as a shield against prosecution.'

'Do you believe that?' I asked.

'Frankly, I don't know,' Reston said. 'I don't think anyone knows for certain. All I can say is if Fox aims to convince people of his innocence, he'd better start with the governor.'

I left Reston's office and hurried back to the boardinghouse. Reston was right. I was certain John Fox would for once agree with his old enemy. The real problem was how to get from this mining camp to the governor's office alive.

A cold wind had picked up while I had been in Reston's office. The wind was rapidly bringing the clouds overhead to a boil. Even as I crossed Carbonate Street on the way to the boardinghouse, snowflakes were whipped through the air. My thoughts were far ahead of my body, and when I walked into the room in the boardinghouse, I felt sudden confusion. Casey was gone.

On top of the dresser I found a note:

Ben,
    I've gone to the bank to speak to Walter. I'll return soon. Wait here for me.
Love,
Casey

I left the boardinghouse on the run and was nearly trampled by the team of an ore wagon as I recrossed Carbonate Street. The teamster cursed me. I stumbled on and ran blindly to the bank. Through the plate-glass window I caught a glimpse of the scene in the bank lobby. Reston and Taylor stood close together. Casey was several paces away, holding her hands to her face. I rushed in and went to her.

Reston said to me, 'You'd better get her out of here, Benjamin. She just threatened to kill Walter.'

Walter Hayes Taylor was pale. He stared at Casey, but I wondered if he actually saw her. He seemed preoccupied.

When I hesitated, Reston said again, 'You'd better go. I'll try to do something here.' He barely jerked his head at Taylor.

I took Casey outside. She held my arm tightly. 'I thought I could help, Ben. I thought he'd listen if I asked him to withdraw the reward on John Fox. He said he wouldn't, not for anyone. Oh, Ben, I should have killed him.'

'No, you shouldn't have, Casey,' I said. 'Come on. Put on your warm clothes and get packed. We're leaving.'

After checking out of the boardinghouse we went to the livery stable. I traded my three mules for one saddle horse. The animal was skittish, but seemed healthy. For another five dollars the liveryman sold me an old saddle

199

and bridle.

Casey and I rode out of camp on the road up Stray Horse Gulch. The wind died down. Large snowflakes floated to the earth. As we rode along the trail that led over the summit of Snowshoe Mountain, everything grew strangely quiet. I could see barely a dozen feet in any direction. I began to worry that John Fox would miss us. He had not said exactly where his new hideout was. I looked back at Casey.

'How's your singing voice?'

'What?' she asked.

I said, 'I want you to sing. Loud. Maybe he'll hear us.'

'What should I sing?' Casey asked.

'Surprise me,' I said.

Into the silence of the snowstorm Casey sang 'Rock of Ages' and 'Onward, Christian Soldiers.' Her voice grew hoarse. I joined in with her. And at last we heard a complaint.

'Stop that racket.'

Casey and I looked back. John Fox rode up the trail behind us.

'That racket would curdle milk inside a cow,' John Fox said.

I gave him a brief account of what Reston had said. I left out Casey's confrontation with Walter Hayes Taylor. I was certain Casey did not want to talk about it. Nothing could be gained by going over the incident again.

John Fox looked around. 'If this storm holds, I figure I can follow the railroad tracks below Stump Town right on past Stallcross's men all the way to Denver.'

'That was my thinking, too,' I said.

John Fox looked at me suspiciously.

I said, 'We're coming with you.'

'No, you're not,' he said. 'It's too risky.' He added, 'You'll slow me down.'

'You won't set any speed records in this storm,' I said. 'And you'll need me when you get to Denver. There's still a price on your head. The first time you identify yourself, some fool is likely to start shooting.' The fool I had in mind was a deputy named Frank.

John Fox nodded. He knew I was right. But he said, 'I don't want to pull you two into this.'

Casey said, 'We're not giving you a choice.' She pulled her horse around. 'The sooner we get going, the better.'

John Fox grinned at me. 'That's some woman there, Benjamin.'

The snowstorm held. If anything, it was heavier by the time we skirted Cloud City and Stump Town and struck the railroad tracks half a mile below the smelter town. The snow now covered the ties, making the steel rails appear to have been laid on the snow.

John Fox led us through the pine forest. As we drew closer to the mountains, a gusting wind picked up. The falling snow swirled before us, giving us blinding glimpses of the country around us. Often we were in sight of the railroad tracks on the left, and I began to see the freight road through the trees on the right.

John Fox raised his hand for us to halt. I heard the riders before I saw them through the swirling snow. There were four of them, moving ghostlike along the freight road. One was Wade Gibson.

Gibson and the riders did not see us, but their horses did. One whinnied. Casey's horse answered.

A tense moment passed. The men rode on in the direction of Stump Town without a glance in our direction, and then they were swallowed up in the storm. The hoofbeats of their mounts grew faint and died away.

John Fox looked back at Casey and me. His eyes sparkled with excitement. 'I've seen battles won or lost by the call of one horse to another.'

Farther on we passed the section of railroad track that had been dynamited by the Fox gang. Some repair work had been done on the bed, but the rails had not been laid. The storm must have brought the work to a stop.

Suddenly the mountains loomed ahead, like massive gray shadows set against the white sky. The railroad tracks pulled close to an icy stream as we approached the narrow mouth of the canyon.

202

John Fox raised his hand again. When we stopped, I smelled smoke from a fire.

In a low voice John Fox said, 'Stallcross must have some men ahead.'

'Or maybe they just left,' I said. 'They might have been the four we saw on the road.'

'Maybe,' John Fox said, peering ahead. 'I'll go in for a closer look.' His saddle creaked as he dismounted.

I swung down and said I would go with him. But John Fox handed the reins of his horse to me. 'This is a one-man job.'

Casey dismounted and stretched her legs. We watched John Fox walk slowly ahead, revolver drawn. He was soon out of our sight.

The next sounds we heard were shouts and a gunshot. The shot was thunderously loud in the pressing silence of the snowstorm. Half a dozen more shots quickly followed. Among them was the booming report of a repeating rifle.

Casey's horse reared. She lost hold of the animal and he fled into the trees, stepping on his reins and tossing his head. I gave Casey the reins I held and ran after her horse. I caught him and led him back in time to see John Fox run out of the trees. He rushed to his horse and grabbed his rifle from the saddle scabbard, turned back, and took aim in the direction he had come.

'This damned storm,' John Fox said breathlessly. 'I walked right into them. There were two of them standing around a fire. I winged one of them.'

John Fox looked anxiously around us. As he did so, the wind came up and cleared the air for a moment. The water in the stream boiled past as it rushed out of the canyon ahead. On the other side I saw a forest of lodgepole pines.

'We can cross here,' John Fox said. 'If we hurry, we can get past those two men before they get brave enough to come looking for us.'

We mounted and moved fast, splashing across the icy stream. John Fox, rifle in hand, led the way and at once looked back, watching for pursuers. Our horses charged through the trees and suddenly broke into a meadow. Ahead I heard a shout. Through the falling snow I saw three men crouched near a tent. In that instant I recognized one. He was Stallcross. The men fired at us, point blank.

We tried to turn our horses, but the men fired a second volley. John Fox was knocked from the saddle. His hat sailed through the air. Casey's horse had just cleared the trees. I saw the animal falter and stumble and go down. Casey leaped free and rolled into the snow.

Sun King squealed as a bullet grazed his flank. I turned him back toward the men and dug my heels into him. Sun King leaped ahead. I drew my revolver and fired rapidly as I rode the men down.

Sun King tried to take the tent in a jump, but he got no footing in the snow. He came down on the tent, nearly fell, then gained his feet and charged ahead. The three men fled.

The forest loomed ahead. Stallcross ran in front of me. I ran him down before he reached the trees, and I slammed the barrel of my revolver across his head. Stallcross dropped into the snow and lay still.

I turned back, and as soon as I saw John Fox, I knew he was dead. His horse lay dead beside him, riddled with bullet wounds that steamed now. I dismounted and knelt beside John Fox. One side of his face was gone. Large snowflakes gently floated into the ghastly wound, lighting upon bright red blood, and then quickly melting.

In a rage I grabbed his rifle from the snow and turned and fired in the direction of the men who had killed John Fox. I shot back into the trees, then fired across the stream at the others until the weapon was empty. I grasped its hot barrel and flung it toward Stallcross's still form in the meadow.

Casey rushed up behind me and threw her arms around me. 'Ben, no, no . . . no.'

Her voice brought me to my senses. I turned to her. Her forehead was scraped raw from her fall. I asked if she was all right. She nodded.

I looked behind her and was amazed to see Casey's horse standing beside Sun King. The horse had been shot through his ribs, but the wound apparently was not fatal.

I tied Casey's horse to a tree. John Fox's

body was surprisingly light. I picked him up and laid him across Casey's horse. My eye was caught by the gold watch. It had fallen from John Fox's vest pocket and dangled by its chain. I took it loose and handed it to Casey. Then I ran a rope beneath the horse and over John Fox's body and tied it.

Casey rode double with me. Leading her horse, we rode back to Cloud City and got away from the mouth of the canyon before Stallcross's men had time to mount an attack.

CHAPTER TWENTY-THREE

Cloud City was in the clouds. The storm seemed to have passed. The snow stopped, but the misty clouds sank to the earth like ghosts.

There was no traffic on Carbonate Street, and few people walked along the boardwalks. Those who did turned to watch Casey and me and the body on the horse we led. I stopped Sun King in front of Taylor's bank.

Casey looked at me as I helped her down. A question was on her face, but she did not voice it. Several people stopped on the boardwalk and looked at me. I untied John Fox's body and lifted him from the saddle. The people parted when I carried the body to the bank door. I nodded for Casey to open it.

The few bank customers and employees

watched in stunned silence as I carried the body to the middle of the lobby and set it on the tiled floor. I looked around.

'Get Taylor.'

Someone already had. A door opened at the rear of the lobby. Walter Hayes Taylor strode past the tellers before he saw what everyone else was looking at. He stopped.

'Good lord!' Taylor began to back away, his eyes fixed on the corpse as though magnetized. I went after him.

No one interfered when I reached Taylor and grasped the lapel of his expensive suit coat and drew him near the body of John Fox. Taylor resisted, but he was not strong. I forced him to his knees and grabbed his beard so he could not look away.

'Keep your eyes open, Taylor,' I said. 'I want you to look. Look long and hard. You offered fifty thousand dollars for John Fox. Here he is. You bought his death.'

The front door opened. Marshal Coe and a deputy came toward us. I turned Taylor loose. He struggled to his feet, looked wild-eyed at Coe, then backed away and retreated into his office.

Coe demanded to know what had happened. I told him. Coe looked down at the body.

'That's Fox? Who killed him?'

'I don't know,' I said. Casey and I went to the door. Marshal Coe called after me.

'I want a statement from you,' he said.

I nodded. 'I'll talk to you tomorrow.'

Outside, Casey and I walked into the misting clouds. We led the horses to the livery. The liveryman examined the wounds. He said Sun King's was minor, but Casey's horse would have to be destroyed.

Casey and I took a room in a nearby boardinghouse. That night I felt exhausted, but I slept little. I had many futile thoughts and waking dreams of the tragedy, trying to think what I could have done to have prevented it.

And during that night I thought back over my life. Since learning the truth of my birth from John Fox, I found I could examine my life in a new way. I realized now that Judge Madison had lived with a dark secret all the time I was growing up. Perhaps he thought he was making up for an injustice by helping raise me and by educating me. He gave me everything but his name.

My mother had lived with the secret, too. Yet in her last hours she must have known that a lie cannot be lived with forever. Her legacy was to send me on a search in the West that would lead me to the truth. In her last hours, perhaps, her conscience was cleared.

I came to know John Fox in the opposite way that I had known Judge Madison. Judge Madison was a man of words. John Fox was a man of action. It was only after John Fox's acceptance of the amnesty agreement that I knew how deeply dissatisfied he was with the life he had led for eighteen years. His written message to the governor shouted of his desire to be freed from his past.

Morning broke under a clear sky. A foot of snow lay on the ground. Casey and I went to breakfast in a cafe on Carbonate Street. Marshal Coe must have had someone watching us. We had taken the day's first scalding sip of coffee when Coe entered the cafe. He came straight to our table, still limping from the leg wound he had received after the robbery of Taylor's bank.

I invited Coe to sit at the table with us. Then I told him in detail what had happened yesterday.

Coe said, 'Stallcross is still laid out on the bunk in the doctor's office. The doctor thinks he's got a busted skull and won't let him move none.'

'Does Stallcross remember what happened?' I asked.

'Seems to,' Coe said. 'He don't think much of you.'

'He should,' I said. 'I could have killed him. He did his best to murder all of us.'

'Well, that's your side of the story,' Coe said. 'Stallcross claims he was apprehending a criminal and you folks got in the road.'

'Do you believe that?' I asked.

'I reckon it doesn't matter what I believe,' Marshal Coe said. 'I'm not placing anybody under arrest.'

Casey said, 'Stallcross should be in jail right now.'

'Some folks would go along with that,' Coe said easily. 'Others figure he's a hero.'

I asked, 'What information did Stallcross have that made him think John Fox would try to escape through the canyon?'

'The way I get it,' Coe said, 'is that Reston told Taylor that Fox was anxious to talk to the governor. Taylor passed that along to Stallcross. Stallcross figured Fox would take the fastest way out of here, and he suspected Fox would use this storm for cover. He's been on Fox's trail long enough to make a close guess at what he was likely to do.'

Marshal Coe looked uneasy. 'There's something else I want to talk to you about.' He paused. 'It's ... delicate.'

'What is it?' I asked.

'Well,' Coe said slowly, 'are you sure that body you brung in is Fox? The way he was shot, it's plumb hard to tell.'

'That was John Fox,' I said. 'Take my word for it.'

'That's good enough for me,' Marshal Coe said. 'But it might not satisfy some folks.'

Casey asked, 'What are you talking about, Marshal?'

'Well, there's a dozen men beating a path to Taylor's door,' Coe said. 'Every one claims he killed John Fox. You never got a look at the man who done it, did you?'

'No,' I said.

Casey shook her head when Coe looked at her.

'Did Stallcross do it?' Coe asked.

'I don't know,' I said. I added, 'It's probably a good thing I don't know.'

'I understand your feelings,' Marshal Coe said. 'Well, I don't see no end to this problem. Plenty of men are going to be hounding Taylor for that money.'

Coe paused. 'There's a story going around now that John Fox ain't dead at all. The story goes that he pulled off this big bank robbery, then he tried to make it look like he was killed, and all the time he's off somewheres living like a king. Some folks just ain't going to believe John Fox is dead.'

At noon that day we buried John Fox in the Cloud City cemetery. The grave was dug into the frozen earth beside the grave of Casey's father. Many sightseers came to the services. Maude was there, dressed in black with a black veil over her face. Surprisingly, Reston came, too. After the burial he told me to meet him at his office.

'We have nothing to talk about,' I said.

'I think we do—'

I interrupted him. 'Reston, you're going to have to get it through your head that you don't own me. I'm not one of your hirelings who jumps to your call.'

'I know you aren't,' Reston said. 'That's

211

what I like about you. You're the kind of young man I'd like to have work with me, not for me. I want you to consider that.'

'No,' I said. I added, 'I'm sorry, Mr Reston. I've come to believe you're a good man. Under different circumstances, I would consider your offer.'

Reston nodded and said he understood. He held his hand out to shake. 'You're an interesting young man, Benjamin. I think you'll go far in whatever you choose to do. May I ask what your plans are?'

I shook his hand, then put my arm around Casey. 'We're leaving Cloud City before the snow gets any deeper.'

'Today?' he asked.

'Just as soon as I can get a horse for Casey,' I said.

'You know, I have a horse that once belonged to John Fox,' Reston said. 'I want to present him to you. Will you take him?'

Casey and I looked at one another. 'Yes, sir,' I said. 'We sure will take him.'

Reston said he would leave the horse tied at the rail behind his office. Casey and I could come and get him any time. He turned away and walked back down the hillside toward camp.

Reston did not follow up on his question about my plans for the future. The matter had troubled me. That day I had no clearer view into the future than I had ever had, but now the

212

question did not bother me so much. I had confidence in myself. And Casey was with me. I knew I could face the future, no matter what changes time brought.

For time brought many changes that no one could have foreseen. The stories of John Fox being alive continued for many years. Stories found their way into books, some claiming that John Fox owned a great ranch somewhere. No one was able to say where. From time to time men claimed to see John Fox at rodeos and horse races in various towns in the West. The fact that Walter Hayes Taylor never paid the fifty-thousand-dollar reward added strength to these yarns.

The next decade brought a radical change. The Silver Panic of 1893 left Walter Hayes Taylor penniless. Taylor, with his domineering wife, lived out his remaining years in a tarpaper shack near Denver. Newspapers reported that the man who was once one of the wealthiest men in the United States could now be found panning gold in a creek that ran past his shack.

The Silver Panic left Cloud City an abandoned mining camp high in the Rockies, marked by dilapidated buildings and the cemetery on the hillside. That cemetery at last claimed Reston, too. Three years after Casey and I left Cloud City, he died of what was called 'mountain fever,' or pneumonia.

And the decade of the nineties saw me open a law practice in San Francisco, on the opposite shore of the continent from where I was raised. I gave the Fox name to Casey, and in time we passed the name on to our children, two boys and a honey-haired girl.

The demands of family and business prevented me from ever seeing Judge Madison again. I looked ahead, with only occasional glances over my shoulder at the past. On the cold, clear day that Casey and I walked down the hill from the Cloud City cemetery, I had already found myself, but I did not know it until I looked back from a distance of many years.

Stephen Overholser was born in Bend, Oregon, the elder son of Western author, Wayne D. Overholser. Convinced, in his words, that 'there was more to learn outside of school than inside,' he left Colorado State College in his senior years to wander. He was drafted and served in the U.S. Army in Vietnam. Following his discharge, he returned to Oregon and launched his career as a writer, publishing three short stories in *Zane Grey Western Magazine*. On a research visit to the University of Wyoming at Laramie, he came across an account of a shocking incident that preceded the Johnson County War in Wyoming in 1892. It was this incident that became the inspiration for his first novel, A HANGING AT SWEETWATER (1974), that received the Golden Spur Award from the Western Writers of America. MOLLY AND THE CONFIDENCE MAN (1975) followed, the first in a series of books about Molly Owens, a clever, resourceful, and tough undercover operative working for a fictional detective agency in the Old West. Among the most notable of Stephen Overholser's later titles are SEARCH FOR THE FOX (1976) and TRACK OF A KILLER (1982). Today he lives in Boulder, Colorado, with his wife and family and in close proximity to his aging father whose most recent Western novel is

215

NUGGET CITY (Five Star Westerns, 1996). Stephen is currently at work on a new Western story, also for Five Star Westerns, titled EMBERS AT DAWN.